James A. Emmerton

A Genealogical Account of Henry Silsbee

And Some of his Descendants

James A. Emmerton

A Genealogical Account of Henry Silsbee
And Some of his Descendants

ISBN/EAN: 9783337144524

Printed in Europe, USA, Canada, Australia, Japan

Cover: Foto ©Raphael Reischuk / pixelio.de

More available books at **www.hansebooks.com**

A

GENEALOGICAL ACCOUNT

OF

HENRY SILSBEE,

AND

SOME OF HIS DESCENDANTS

BY

JAMES A. EMMERTON. M. D.

From Historical Collections of Essex Institute.

SALEM:

ESSEX INSTITUTE.

1880.

HENRY SILSBEE AND SOME OF HIS DESCENDANTS.

THE name of Silsbee is one of the rarest in the records accessible at London. I found but two wills at Somerset House; that of John Scylesbie of the parish of Weston under Weytheley (Camden, ed. 1701, gives Wetherly and Wethley), Warwickshire. He is called "yeoman," died in 1557, and mentions no children nor any relatives of his name, and that of Thomas Sellesby of West Thorocke,[1] Essex, dec'd on or about 8 Sept., 1653 (nuncupative), to brother Matthew Sillsbey one-half of my estate, sister Bethia Marten and her two children the other half. Abdiel Silsbye obtained a license, at Westminster, to marry Anne Alleyne of that place on the 16 February, 1641–2, and was married the same day at St. Margaret's, the parish church so near the Abbey. Even the most recent maps give the name "Silsby Road" to a lane winding about the fields between Shepherd's Bush and Hammersmith; but a visit to the locality, one day in October, 1879, revealed the fact that omnivorous London had pushed out in that direction, and road as well as name were, even then, just disappearing under the rectilinear streets of a new suburb.

The parish-records of Olney, Bucks, dating from about 1666, give baptisms of a Samuel Silsby's daughters after 1670.

Mr. James Stowe, the affable parish-clerk, told me while I was studying the inscriptions on the gravestones

---

[1] West Thurrock is a parish on the left bank of the Thames, nearly opposite Greenwich.

in the churchyard, that the name had disappeared from Olney but still remained in neighboring villages.

Mr. Stowe's interest in such matters was evinced by the care with which he had cleaned the inscriptions obscured by lichen and mold rather than age, for few, if any, antedated the eighteenth century.

The records contain many entries of familiar Lynn names : Laughton, Purryer, Collins, Townsend, Cooper, etc. ; and, though Farrington and Kyrtland had disappeared, I was more than ever inclined to the theory that Henry Sillsbey had moved from Salem and Ipswich to Lynn, in order to be near old-country neighbors.

	BORN.	DIED.	MARRIED.	
1 Henry,	bef. 1618,	1700		Dorothy
			18 Nov., 1680,	Grace Eaton.

By Dorothy he had

	BORN.	DIED.	MARRIED.	
2 Henry,				
3 Nathaniel,	ab' 1651,	ab' 1717,	5, 9, 1671,	Deborah Tompkins.
			before 1697,	Eliz'b Pickering.
4 Mary,			15, 6, 1664,	Zachery Marsh.
5 John,		bef' 26 June, 1676,	15 Feb., 1673,	Bethia Pitman.
6 Jonathan,			1, 11, 1673,	Bethiah Marsh.
7 Samuel,		Oct. 1687,	4 July, 1676,	Mary Biscoe.
8 Ephraim,		bef' Mch, 1729,	23 Jan., 1693,	Rachel Bassett.
9 Hannah,		8 Jan., 1682,	2 Dec., 1680,	Thos. Laughton, Jr.
10 Sarah (?),			25 Feb., 1682,	Joseph Collins.

"25 day of the 5ᵗʰ moneth 1639 Henry Sillsby Mr. Sharpes man is receaued an Inhabitant within this Jurisdicion, & ther is graunted to him halfe an acre of land neere the Cat Coue for a howse plott" IX,89[2]. This is the first appearance of the name on our (Salem) records. Mr. Samuel Sharpe came to Salem in 1629, and, if Henry came with him as his "man," we must antedate by some ten years the birth-date assumed above which is based upon the supposition that he was at least of age in 1639.

[2] In this paper, references like IX,89 are to volume and page of the Historical Collections of the Essex Institute.

Savage says he was of Ipswich in 1647.

On the "16 Oct. 1651 Henry Silsby of Ipswich buys of Obediah Flud of Boston and Thomas Coats of Lynn the now dwelling house of Thomas Coates in Linn, once in the occupation of Joseph Flud, with six acres of ground next the little river east and west upon Town Common, S' by Edw'd Ierson and N' by Robert Rand." The "little river" is Stacy's Brook, which crosses the Eastern railroad a short distance southwest of the Swampscott station. The Coates house was on what is now Fayette street a few doors east of Essex street. On the same day, in 1651, Silsbee bought some thirty acres of arable and pasture land, apparently not far from the home-lot, and on the 7 April, 1660, he bought of John Hathorne an old house and three acres bounded west with his own land.

16 March, 1670–1, the town had bought of Robert Rand the land bounding the Coates home-lot on the north, and, reserving three poles in width along its northern side for the road to Marblehead (Essex street), the selectmen sold the rest to Henry Silsbee "shooemaker" in consideration of a similar three pole strip from his own land next east, and eight pounds sterling to them in hand paid.

This estate, comprising a large part of the level land on the right between the hills near the Swampscott station and the first over-head bridge on the way to Lynn by the Eastern railroad, is still cultivated in part by **148** Henry Otis Silsby.

1 HENRY was never very prominent in town affairs, but his name occurs frequently as witness, overseer or assessor in the wills of his neighbors.

8 Jan., 1692, Voted, that * * * Henry Silsbee * * * should sit in the deacon's seat.[3]

---

3 Hist. Lynn, p. 292.

In his will, signed **17** March, 1698–9, and proved 16 Dec., 1700, he calls himself "aged and weak."

Dorothy, the mother of his children, died 27 Sep., 1676. Grace Eaton, who is not mentioned in **1** Henry's will, was widow of Jonas of Reading.[4]

Lewis supposes that the Henry who married in 1680 was a son of the first settler, but I find in a ledger of Capt. Geo. Corwin of Salem, certain sales "to his sone Eaton" charged to **1** Henry and acknowledged on squaring accounts, as was the fashion of those times, by his unmistakable and unusually legible signature, Henery Sillsbey.

2 HENRY (**1** Henry). I have found no other trace of this son Henry than the fact that **1** Henry is called Senior in Corwin's Ledger in 1678.

3 NATHANIEL, Salem (**1** Henry).

	BORN.	DIED.	MARRIED.	
3 Nathaniel,	ab' 1651,	ab' 1717, 18,	5, 9, 1671,	Deborah Tompkins.
			& 2ndly	
			bef. 1697,	Eliz^h Pickering.
By Deborah				

	BORN.	DIED.	MARRIED.	
11 Henry,	12 Ap., 1674,			
12 Nathaniel,	11, 2, 1676,	21, 2, 1676.		
13 Nathaniel,	23, 8, 1677,	2 Jan., 1769,	27 May, 1703,	Hannah Pickering.
			before 1715,	Martha ——
14 Samuel,	30 Jan., 1679,			
15 John,	20 M'ch, 1682,			
16 Margaret,	20 M'ch, 1684,		29 M'ch, 1711,	Ephraim Skerry.
By Elizabeth				
17 Elizabeth,	bpd. at age } 11 Feb., 1710, }		10 Feb., 1720-1,	Jno. Cavies of Ips'h.
18 Mary,				
19 Sarah,				
20 Jonathan,			12 Ap., 1720,	Abigail White.
21 Hannah,			?26 J'ly, 1721,	Jona' Felt.
22 Jane,			?2 Jan., 1734,	John Flint.
23 Ann,		b'd Dec., 1723.		
24 Abigail,				
25 Benjamin,		bef' 1754,		Mary.
26 William,				
27 Joseph,			23 Dec., 1735,	Mary Pain.
			25 Jan., 1743,	Marg^t Abbott.

[4] Hist. Reading, Mass., p. 63.

3 March, 1706, Nathaniel deposes that upwards of forty years before he was an apprentice of John Symonds, of Salem, who lived in North-fields. Here he found his wife Deborah, baptized 8, 4, 1651, died before 1697, a daughter of John Tompkins who was son of Ralph. John Tompkins came to this country so early that on 20, 1, 1636, he is promised that he will be received an inhabitant of Salem "in case he procure free dismission" (from some other church), IX,41,51. 12, 5, 1637, this promise is fulfilled and land is granted to him. After the death of Margaret, the mother of his children, he married, September, 1673, Mary Read. On 1 July, 1675, he and w' Mary sold to Joseph and Benjamin Pope thirty acres, granted to him by the town, bounded by land of said Popes easterly, and by the Ipswich river northerly. He died in 1681.

Ralph, then fifty years old, came over in the Truelove, Captain Gibbs, in 1635, with wife Catherine fifty-eight, Samuel twenty-two, Elizabeth eighteen, and Marie fourteen. Hist. and Gen. Reg., XIV,323.

Savage says he was freeman of Dorchester, 2 May, 1638. Land is granted to him in Salem in 1642 and afterwards. Toward the close of his life, his, then recently deceased, wife (probably a second wife who had been a widow Foster) is called sister by Samuel Eborne, who calls himself about fifty years old in 1670.

On the 22 April, 1659, Ralph Tompkins, planter, sells to Edward Gaskill, ship carpenter, about a half-acre and a dwelling-house, formerly the dwelling of John Hart "near the tide-mill and Strong-water brook," and therefore near the corner of Grove and Main streets, Peabody. After the death of his wife he removed to Bridgewater to live with his son Samuel.

On file at our Court-house are several depositions, unfortunately without date, in regard to the expressed wishes of the old couple that their little property might be given to one Mary Foster, in requital of her assiduous care of their feeble old age. In this connection Ralph speaks of his "son Foster." In effect their wishes were carried out, although the son and admn'r John inherited the land. I notice that when Nathaniel Silsbee, senior, sells in 1697 and 1703 certain small lots of land in North-fields, the owners of the adjoining lots bear much the same names that appear in the above-named depositions.

22 March, 1671–2, "Its left to the Selectmen to sell house-lotts in the swampy land in the comon * * * to such persons as shall need them provided they build houses on them in two years time." Under this vote the town sold the lots fronting on Essex street between New-bury and Pleasant streets.

That **3** Nathaniel improved his, which was at or near the site of the Phillips school-house, appears from his joining with his neighbors in an agreement about the common-drain in 1700.

"Salem-Towne is debtor, 27, 3, 1677, to Nathaniel Silsbee for altering "ye fore seat" in the Meeting-house." (Cap't George Corwin's ledger.)

20 Aug., 1684, Nathaniel, with his neighbor Peter Cheever, glover, buys of Samuel Williams four acres of that "land in North-fields" which we shall trace from generation to generation for one hundred and fifty years.

If there is any foundation for the family tradition that one of the name made the coffins which his son took to Gallows Hill for the executed witches of 1692, it must refer to this Nathaniel. He and many of the name after him were joiners, housewrights, or carpenters.

27 Feb., 1697–8, Nath's wife Elizabeth surrenders her right of dower in a piece of land in North-field, which he sells to David Foster.

10 Jan., 1700–1, Jonathan Pickering of Salem, shipwright, gives a power of attorney to Nath¹ Silsby, of Salem, joyner, his son-in-law.

30 M'ch, 1715, Elizabeth Silsby and the other Pickering heirs release to Jona' Glover their claim to real estate in South-field which their father, Jonathan Pickering, sells to him. Jonathan Pickering, born in Salem, 1639, son of John the founder of that well-known family, and his wife Elizabeth, married 19 M'ch, 1665–6, Jane, dau. of Doctor Thomas Cromwell and his wife Ann. They had, among others, Elizabeth, born 2 June, 1669, and Hannah, baptized 28 May, 1682.

The town-record of the children of **3** Nathaniel and Deborah stops with Margaret. The next dau. Elizabeth, though baptized at age the same day as Margaret, is not married till nine years later; all the younger children receive Pickering names. I venture to begin the list of the second wife's children with her namesake Elizabeth.

Nath¹ Silsbee, sen., is taxed 26 Aug., 1717, and his widow from 17 Sept., 1718. His inventory, taken by Joseph Andrews, Miles Ward and Benj. Ives, is presented by his son, **13** Nathaniel, admn'r 3 July, 1724. It includes house, barn, about thirty poles of land and a common right, about nine acres in North-field and two and a half in Ferry lane. Total £219. 13. 00.

By an account of administration, rendered 3 Jan., 1728–9, and accompanying papers it appears that two of the sons had been recently at school, and that "our Mother" and sister Ann had died, apparently in the winter of 1723–4. 2 Jan'y, 1728, Ben^a Smith receipts to the administrator for the interest his (Smith's) wife had in the Ferry-lane property.

The estate is to be divided among fifteen children, but since the list includes Ann, known to be dead, we can draw no safe inference that the others were still living, especially since the same list, except Ann and Benjamin who is represented by heirs, is used 23 Jan'y, 1755, when the division really takes place and the admn'r acknowledges that he is the sole surviving son.

Of all the large family of **3** Nathaniel very little nametrace remains except of his descendants through **13** Nathaniel, his eldest and finally only surviving son; **11** Henry does not appear on the list of heirs, 1728; of **14** Samuel I find no trace whatever; of **15** John one of the name is warned for military duty 23 Aug., 1703, and is taxed for 1705–8, but all these things may apply to **28** John. **20** Jonathan is taxed in 1719–22 and married 12 April, 1720. His widow Abigail is called "chocolate-grinder, 3 Feb., 1757, when her brother John White, mariner, sells to her his right in their paternal estate on Essex street nearly opposite the residence of **13** Nathaniel.

25 Benjamin appears on the tax-list 1726–45. He married Mary ———— and had Mary, born 25 Oct., 1733; Benjamin, 26 June, 1738; and Sarah, 8 June, 1742. One John Booth marries Mary Silsbee 28 Feb., 1749–50, and, 27 Dec., 1753, is appointed guardian to Benjamin Silsbee, minor, upwards of fourteen years. Sureties, Benj. Porter of Danvers and Thos. Downing of Lynn, and the latter, or one of his name, had married, 16 Dec., 1753–4, Mary Silsbee perhaps the daughter. In 1781 I find land near Stage-point in South Salem bounded by land of Benj. Sylsbe, and 3 Aug., 1781, Enoch James of Boston, blacksmith, is allowed as guardian unto Benjamin Silsby and Dorcas Silsby above fourteen years, and to Polly and Nabby, minors, under fourteen,— children of Benjamin Silsby, late of Boston, Cooper. Sureties, David Bell, gent[n], and Francis James, bricklayer.[5]

26 William and **27** Joseph were, I suppose, the pupils of Master Swinnerton, about 1728–9. I find but one William on the town tax-list, but in the East church records W[m] and W[m], Jun., in 1757–8. **27** Joseph married 23 Dec., 1735, Mary Pain, and had a dau. Elizabeth, bp'd 28 Nov., 1736.

Joseph married again 25 Jan., 1743, Margaret Abbott who survived him, married in 1770 John Young, and died 1 March, 1809, aged ninety.

1741, Mr. Jos. Silsby gives 15s. towards the bell on St. Peter's, II,258.

4 MARY, Salem (**1** Henry) married 15, 6, 1664, Zachery Marsh, bp'd 30 April, 1637, a son of John and Susanna who came to Salem (Savage "doubts not") in 1634. They had John born 26 Sept., 1665, Mary, 8 Dec., 1666, Zachariah, Elizabeth, Jonathan born 14 April, 1672, married 1697 Mary Very, born 1668, dau. of Samuel and Alice (Woodice) II,35, and Ebenezer born 28 May, 1674.

5 JOHN, Salem (**1** Henry) married 15 Feb., 1673, Bethia dau. of Nathaniel Pitman. They had but one son **28** John, born 7 Feb., 1674. The father died before 26 June, 1676, when his inventory amounted to £74. 16s. His widow married 15 Dec., 1680, Alexander Coale of Marblehead. Coale died before 24 Aug., 1687, when his will dated 24 June, 3rd James II, was proved. In it he leaves £20 to his son John Silsby, and mentions son

---

[5] Adm'n to Mary widow of Benj. Silsby, 12 Feb., 1793. Wyman " Gen. and Est., of Charlestown."

Alex. Coale, wife Bethia and sisters Anna and Jannett Coale of Dumbarton, Scotland.

6 JONATHAN, Lynn (1 Henry).

	BORN.	DIED.	MARRIED.	
6 Jonathan,			1, 11, 1673,	Bethia Marsh.

They had

	BORN.	DIED.	MARRIED.	
29 A child,	16, 12, 1676,	16, 12, 1676,		
30 Jonathan,	16 M'ch, 1677-8,		1700.	Elizh Collins.
31 Sarah,	5, 10, 1674,		9 Sept., 1707,	Geo. Lilly.
32 Bethiah,	12 Apr., 1680,	16 May, 1681,		
33 Elizabeth,	2 Aug., 1685,			
34 Hannah,	3 Oct., 1687,	ab' 1759,	15 M'ch, 1710,	Samuel Abbe.

In 1698 it appears by the will of 1 Henry, who bequeaths him the lot, that Jonathan had been for some years improving "four acres next ye lane and Benj. Farr's hill." This may well have been the lot which Henry bought in 1660 of John Hathorne, and the old house, mentioned at that time, was perhaps "my old dwelling-house and barn" which Jonathan sells, 25 Dec., 1708, to Ephraim Stasey, with four acres bounding "North on the country-road leading to Marblehead."

On the 13 Dec., 1708, Jonathan Silsbee, husbandman, and wife, Bethiah, sell to Henry Collins, jun., land "near my now dwelling-house" bounding east on Benjamin Farr.

These sales of the family houses and lands receive an explanation in the statement of Jonathan, jun., which may be found on our Court Records in 1709, that he and his father and George Lilly[6] are about removing out of the province.

In Larned's "Windham County, Conn.," pp. 274–9, I find a Jonathan Silsbee, active in the formation, in October, 1731, of Scotland parish, and, in 1740, assigned to a front seat in the new meeting-house.

---

[6] George Lilley, of Lynn, also appears in the early Windham records.

In Weaver's "Windham" p. 17, I find the marriage of
a Hannah which I have ventured to insert in the family
table and, on page 67, that Chloe, a dau. of John Silsbee,
married 27 Sept., 1774, Deacon Samuel Baker and died
29 Sept., 1778, aged forty.

Emigration from this part of Connecticut to Brimfield,
Mass., carried thither many of our local surnames and I
have little doubt that the occurrence of the name of
Silsbee in those parts may be thus accounted for.

Bethia Marsh was a sister of Zachery, p. ~~285~~.*//*.

7 SAMUEL, Lynn (**1** Henry) married 4 July, 1676,
Mary Biscoe and was buried 18 Oct., 1687. They had
one child, **35** Mary, born 20 June, 1677. His inventory
taken 12 March, 1687–8, shows a small property with no
real estate.

Suffolk Prob., B. 13, p. 21, mentions the brothers
Nathaniel, Ephraim and Jonathan, and Mary Johnson
admn'x of her late husband Samuel Silsbee dec'd.

The Lynn Town-records give us the publishment of
Mary Silsbee to Nathaniel Collins, both of Lynn, 27
March, 1699, VI,79.

8 EPHRAIM, Lynn (**1** Henry).

	BORN.	DIED.	MARRIED.	
8 Ephraim,		bef' M'ch, 1729,	23 Jan., 1693,	Rachel Bassett.

	BORN.	DIED.	MARRIED.	
36 Henry,	15 Nov., 1694,	Dec., 1761,	3 Dec., 1713,	Abigail Collins.
37 Ephraim,				Esther Southwick.
38 Rachel.				

In his father's will Ephraim, although judging from the
date of his marriage, much the youngest son, gets the
paternal homestead and neighboring land. Nathaniel had
settled in Salem and inherited money but no land, and
Jonathan had been already provided with house and land.

Perhaps to balance the unequal division of the real-estate the payment of Nathaniel's legacy rests with Ephraim, but he shares with Jonathan in paying the other legacies and they divide the "movables" equally.

Ephraim left no will. A committee appointed to divide the estate makes careful provision for the widow, but declares it impossible to make further division without injury.

Rachel Bassett, dau. of William and Sarah, dau. of Hugh Burt, was born 13 March, 1666.

William Bassett, Lynn, 1640, died 31 March, 1703, is prominent in the earliest records of Lynn. As Ensign, in the company of Captain Joseph Gardner of Salem, he was in the swamp-fight, of 1675 ; as Captain, he was one of a council-of-war at Scarborough, Me., in 1689 ; and is called Quarter-master in 1691. (Hist. Lynn, p. 184.) His dau. Elizabeth had married John Procter of Danvers. Rev. C. W. Upham in his "History of Witchcraft, etc.," Vol. II, p. 312, says, "The bitterness of the prosecutors against Procter was so vehement, that they not only arrested, and tried to destroy, his wife and all his family above the age of infancy, in Salem, but all her relatives in Lynn, many of whom were thrown into prison." Of these her sister-in-law Sarah (Hood) wife of William Bassett, jun., and her sister Mary, widow of Michel Derich, were imprisoned, in Boston, some seven months.

A Rachel Silsbee married 11 Dec., 1729, Benjamin Rhoads, both of Lynn, and had Rachel born 27 Feb., 1731–2, and Benjamin, 11 Sept., 1734.

9 HANNAH (1 Henry).

Hannah married Thomas Laughton, jun., son of the first Thomas. They had but one son, John, born 3 Jan.,

1682, VI,225, and Hist. Lynn, p. 155. The consideration in which the elder Thomas was held is evinced by
his election as Selectman, in 1645, and his appointment,
the same year by the house of deputies at the request of
the town, "to draw wine" and, with Edward Burcham
and Thomas Putnam "to end small controversies." The
next year he was a representative, and (Lewis says)
town-clerk in 1672.

10 SARAH (**1** Henry).

As far as the public records show, Henry Collins, born
23 Nov., 1672, son of Joseph and Sarah, was the only
one of four contemporary Henrys who could have been the
"grandson Henry Collins" of **1** Henry's will.

13 NATHANIEL, Salem (**3** Nathaniel, **1** Henry).

	BORN.	DIED.	MARRIED.	
13 Nathaniel,	23 Oct., 1677,	2 Jan., 1769,	27 May, 1703,	Hannah Pickering.
			secondly	Martha
By Hannah				

	BORN.	DIED.	MARRIED.	
39 Nathaniel,	11 Aug., 1705,	4 Aug., 1734,	24 Oct., 1730,	Mary Daniell.
40 Hannah,	.		pub. 29 June,	Joseph Prince.
			1729. 2ndly	
			26 Oct., 1730,	John Mascoll.
By Martha				
41 William,	bpd. 14 Aug., 1715.	ab' J'ly, 1783,	17 Oct., 1735,	Joanna Fowle.

25 Jan., 1700–1, Jeremiah Neale, admn'r to the estate
of Michael Chapleman, sells to Nath¹ Silsbee, jun., his
dwelling-house and about twelve poles of land, bounded
northerly on the highway, *etc.*

This house, still standing on Essex street (No. 69 on
the atlas of 1874), nearly opposite Pleasant street, remained in the hands of the heirs of his son William until
1797, V,193.

Had always thought that some explanation was needed
of the fact that Hannah Silsbee did not join her sister

Eliz'h Silsbee and the other heirs of Jona' Pickering in their release to Jona' Glover, 30 Mar., 1715. See p. ~~263~~.

The Records of the First Church inform me that *Martha*, wife of Nathaniel Silsbee, had renewed her covenant and had her child baptized on the 14 Aug., 1715.

7 July 1728, Martha, wife of Nathaniel Silsby, and Anstis, wife of John Crowninshield, request a recommendation to the East Parish. Have been unable to determine her surname.

Nathaniel's will dated 31 March, 1760, and admitted to probate 7 Feb., 1769, gives "to grandson Samuel, son of my son Nathaniel, deceased, seven acres of my land in North-field in my nine-acre lot formerly belonging to my father deceased;" to daughter Hannah Mascoll £26. 13. 4. and to son William, who is to be executor, the rest.

36 HENRY, Lynn (8 Ephraim, 1 Henry).

	BORN.	DIED.	MARRIED.	
36 Henry,	15 Nov., 1694,	Dec., 1761,	3 Dec., 1713,	Abigail Collins.
They had				

	BORN.	DIED.	MARRIED.	
42 Daniel,		1769,		Patience
43 Samuel,		27 J'ly, 1798,		Sarah Breed.
44 Lydia,				Aholiab Dimond.
45 Miriam,			8 Dec, 1741,	Nehemh Collins.
46 Henry,	25 Jan., 1731,	Aug. 1803,		Hannah Bassett.

Henry, husbandman, inherited the homestead and added greatly to the real estate. His will dated 10, 11, 1761, mentions the children as above and grandson Sampson Silsbee. His inventory, 2 April, 1762, by Wm Zachery and Jedidiah Collins includes more than 150 acres. Among the personals, mention is made of "Delph ware." (His father's and grandfather's inventories have no earthen vessels.) Certain furniture is located in "the old part of the house."

The son Daniel files an objection to the probate of the will, but it is set up with Henry for sole-executor and residuary legatee.

37 EPHRAIM, Boston (**8** Ephraim, **1** Henry).
B. 78, **f.** 164. Ephraim Silsbee, of Boston, blacksmith, and wife, Esther, sell, 23, 4, 1739, to our brother Daniel Southwick, of Salem, tanner, all our share of houses and land and all our portion belonging to us of our father Lawrence Southwick and our mother Tamson Southwick estate.

12 March, 1764, Daniel, of Boston, innholder, made "my uncle Ephraim Silsbe of Boston, shipwright, and son Daniel, executors." It appears that Ephraim "renounced" the office.

39 NATHANIEL, Salem (**13** Nath¹, **3** Nath¹, **1** Henry).

	BORN.	DIED.	MARRIED.	
39 Nathaniel,	11 Aug., 1705,	4 Aug., 1734,	24 Oct., 1730,	Mary Daniell.
	They had			
47 Samuel.	15 Nov., 1731,	14 Dec., 1803,	22 Jan., 1756,	Martha Prince.
48 Nathaniel,	26 Dec., 1733,	early.		

1731, J. Higginson sold to N. Silsbee, jun., the estate on the western corner of Daniels and Essex street. 4 Aug., 1734, Nathaniel was at work outside of a large building when the staging fell and he alone, of a working-party of twenty-five carpenters, lost his life; the others escaped by jumping in at the windows.

16 March, 1748, Stephen Daniell (XIV,252) gives to his daughter Mary Silsbey, widow, a quarter-acre, dwelling-house, barn, *etc.*, "where I now dwell." This was the lot, on the opposite corner of Daniels street, which Stephen had bought on the 9 March, 1692, a few months previous to his marriage, of Joseph Grafton, jun.

2

Here the widow passed the rest of her life, helping out her narrow income by the profits of a small shop, and here her descendants dwelt for more than a hundred years.

In 1754, Mary Silsbey and Samuel sell their old home, across the way, to E. Whittemore, who then occupied it.

41 WILLIAM, Salem (13 Nath¹, 3 Nath¹, 1 Henry).

	BORN.	DIED.	MARRIED.	
41 William,	bp'd 14 Aug., 1715,	ab' J'ly, 1783,	17 Oct., 1735,	Joanna Fowle.
They had				
	BORN.	DIED.	MARRIED.	
49 Nathaniel,	9 Nov., 1748,	25 June, 1791,	1 Nov., 1770,	Sarah Becket.
50 Martha,			pub' 19 Sep ,	Wm Emmerton.
			1761. 2ndly	Christ Babbadge.
51 Joanna,			pub'22 Oct.,	Mansfield Burrill.
			1763.	
52 Hannah,				Elijah Haskell.
53 William (?),	ab' 1749,	July, 1791.		

William was a carpenter. He brings a bill for labor on the East church during the repairs in 1766. His will, dated October, 1778, and admitted to probate 10 July, 1783, gives everything to wife Joanna, whom he makes executrix. He lived on Essex street opposite Pleasant. There is no inventory. The mention of "two acres in Ferry-lane" in the inventory of another William Silsbee (called junior, aged forty-five in the Town Record of his death), deceased, intestate in 1794, and his estate administered by Mansfield Burrill, so strongly suggest a family connection that I have ventured to insert his name.

Joanna Fowle, born about 1713, died 25 Feb., 1793, was dau. of Zechary, born 7 Sept., 1676, died 10 Jan., 1718, and married 21 Nov., 1700, Ruth (Ingersoll) ; he a son of Zecharias, died 7 Jan., 1678, and Mary (Paine) ; he a son of George, born about 1610, of Concord and Charlestown, died 19 Sept., 1682, and Mary born about 1614, died 15 Feb., 1676.

42 DANIEL, Boston (36 Henry, 8 Ephraim, 1 Henry).

	BORN.	DIED.	MARRIED.	
42 Daniel,		ab' 1769,		Patience
They had				

	BORN.	DIED.	MARRIED.	
54 Daniel,		1791,		
55 Sampson,		bef' May, 1824,	24 Sept., 1772,	Abigail Collins
56 Abner,		? bef' Jan., 1770,		
57 Sarah,		ab' 1808,	unmarried,	
58 Abigail,		ab' 1815,	unmarried,	
59 Mary,				Ezra Curtain.

In 1755 Daniel is called shipwright. In the settlement of his estate he is called innholder on Prince street (see Wyman "Gen. and Est., of Charlestown," II,865). His will dated 12 March, 1764, and admitted to probate 31 Oct., 1769, mentions his family as above. In the partition of the estate, 24 Jan., 1770, no mention is made of Abner.

26 Aug., 1808, Sarah and Abigail devise their property to one another, except that Sarah leaves a portion to Sampson. Sarah's will comes to probate on the 20 Oct., following, but Abigail's not until 24 July, 1815.

43 SAMUEL, Lynn (36 Henry, 8 Ephraim, 1 Henry).

	BORN.	DIED.	MARRIED.	
43 Samuel,		27 July, 1798,		Sarah Breed.
They had				

	BORN.	DIED.	MARRIED.	
60 Lydia,	20 Oct., 1755,	Jan 1806,	unmarried,	
61 Sarah,	4 June, 1758,	3 Dec., 1829,		Stephen Smith.
62 Hannah,	29 Mc'h, 1760,	7 Aug., 1842,	unmarried,	
63 Henry,	12 J'ly, 1762,	5 Aug., 1821,		Sarah Phillips.
64 Samuel,	4 Jan., 1765,			Sarah Breed.
65 Nehemiah,	12 J'ly, 1768,	3 May, 1832,		Elizb Breed.
66 Abigail,	27 Oct., 1771,	30 Dec., 1818,	unmarried.	

Samuel is called shipwright. He had in 1796 a mansion in Blackmarsh, as the lower end of Union street, near the water, was called, where he had bought land of the town in 1766. He built many schooners for the fishermen of Marblehead. His widow died 9 Dec., 1809.

60 Lydia. Her will is dated 31, 8, 1805. Her estate, inventoried the next October, amounted to $2,387.50.

66 Abigail. 16 Feb., 1849, the next of kin convey, in accordance with a wish expressed in her last sickness, certain real estate which she and her sister, **62** Hannah, had received by will of their late father Samuel.

44 LYDIA, Lynn (**36** Henry, **8** Ephraim, **1** Henry).

44 Lydia was published, 21 Sept., 1735, to Aholiab Diamond son of John. They were married and had Samuel, Richard, who died in 1768, and Mary who, marrying 2 Oct., 1760, Robert Pitcher, became the well-known Moll Pitcher. An interesting sketch of this famous woman may be found in Lewis's History of Lynn, pp. 374–6.

45 MIRIAM, Lynn (**36** Henry, **8** Ephraim, **1** Henry).

45 Miriam married 8 Dec., 1741, Nehemiah Collins and had Abijah born 27 March, 1742, Nathaniel born 28 Nov., 1745, married Elizabeth Phillips, Abigail born 23 Feb., 1748, married 24 Sept., 1772, her cousin **55** Sampson Silsbee, Ruth born 3 Dec., 1750, married —— Hawks, Martha born 6 Feb., 1757 (N. S.), married —— Green, of Seabrook, Me., and Micajah born 30 July, 1759, lost at sea.

Nehemiah Collins was a son of Nathaniel, born 29 Apr., 1689, and Charity —— ; he a son of Henry, born 2 Oct., 1651, and Sarah (Heires) ; he a son of Henry born about 1630, died 12 Oct., 1722, and Mary dau. of Thomas Tolman, an early settler of Dorchester; and he a son of Henry Collins who, with wife Ann, three children and five servants came over in the Abigail in 1635.

46 Henry, Lynn (36 Henry, 8 Ephraim, 1 Henry).

	BORN.	DIED.	MARRIED.
46 Henry,	25 Jan., 1731,	Aug., 1803,	Hannah Bassett.

They had

	BORN.	DIED.	MARRIED.
67 Henry,	24 Apr., 1775,	30 July, 1844,	Mary Chase.
			Miriam Gould.
68 Hannah,	24 Apr., 1775,	1 Mc'h, 1842,	Benjamin Dow.
69 Daniel,	12 May, 1777,	24 Jan., 1840,	Lydia Curtin.
			Lydia Nichols.
			Sally (Curtin) Burrill.
70 Abigail,	5 June, 1779,	5 July, 1812,	James Curtin.

68 Hannah and Benjamin Dow had no children.

70 Abigail and James Curtin had James Albert, who
died unmarried, aged about 19, in 1819, Abigail S., who
died in 1817, aged 18, and Maria, who married Enos
Hoag of North Berwick, Maine.

47 Sam'l, Salem (39 Nath¹, 13 Nath¹, 3 Nath¹, 1 Henry).

	BORN.	DIED.	MARRIED.	
47 Samuel,	15 Nov., 1731,	14 Dec., 1803,	22 Jan., 1756,	Martha Prince.

They had

	BORN.	DIED.	MARRIED.	
71 Nathaniel,			unmarried.	
72 Mary,		single,		
73 Hannah,	ab' 1761,	July, 1793,	1 Nov., 1781,	John McGregor.
74 Samuel,	ab' 1763,	June, 1822,	1 Oct., 1786,	Rebecca Read.
75 Deborah,	19 Apr., 1767,	13 April, 1836,	8 Oct., 1786,	Daniel Sage.
76 Sarah,		early,		
77 Sarah,	ab' 1774,	2 Sept., 1860,	14 Aug., 1803,	David Patten.
			29 Jan., 1808,	Hatfield W. Read.

Samuel was a carpenter. The accounts of the East
Church show his bill for "clabording" in July, 1766.
He probably built the northern part of the house, at the
eastern corner of Daniels and Essex streets, where he
passed his whole life. This wing, although ancient, is
evidently more modern than the rest, and was built, his
daughter Sarah said, "long before her time." He left no
will. His inventory, taken 6 June, 1804, includes about
eleven acres in North-fields.

Martha Prince, born about 1731, died 15 Sept., 1817, XIV,249, is thus noted by Dr. Bentley. "A very pleasant, faithful and worthy woman, very active for her years till near the close of her life, died 15 Sept., 1817, aged 86 ; 24 years old at marriage ; 47 years of married state ; left 3 children. She a daughter of John son of Deacon Richard Prince. Husband died 1803 aged 73. Daniels street in Daniels house corner upon Essex, near meetinghouse. Sara Knight her sister-in-law."

A patient endeavor to reconcile Dr. Bentley's genealogy with the facts results in a conviction that he had trusted his memory too implicitly and should have written "daughter of *Joseph* son of Deacon Richard Prince."

It will be noticed that Dr. Bentley's record makes Martha Prince's birth-date 1731 or 32.

There is no record of marriage of John Prince till he married Hannah Frost 23 Jan., 1734–5, nor of any children except John born 14 Oct., 1735.

Joseph Prince is published to Hannah Silsbee 29 June, 1729.

Hannah Prince witnesses a signature of Deacon Richard 20 Jan., 1735, three days before John married Hannah Frost. Hannah Prince marries John Mascoll 26 Oct., 1739. In 1754 Sarah Mascoll, Martha and Deborah Prince, spinsters, join with John Mascoll, Richard Prince and Elizabeth Prince (dau. of Deacon Richard) in releasing to John and Richard the northern and southern parts, respectively, of Deacon Richard's homestead.

In these deeds I suppose Sarah Mascoll represents her mother Sarah Prince, who married John Mascoll, jun., 12 Aug., 1729, while Martha and Deborah represent their father Joseph. Not till 1760 does John Prince, aforesaid, born 14 Oct., 1735, of Marblehead, appear to release to his uncle Richard all claim to the southern portion of his grandfather, Deacon Richard Prince's homestead.

Family tradition does not oppose this conclusion and adds that the sister Deborah Prince married, 14 Oct., 1755, Samuel Webb, who married again, 9 Nov., 1758, Hannah Ward. A choice which, local gossip says, the practical widower made on the very day of Deborah's funeral.

It will be seen, p. 31, that the children of **75** Deborah, after the first John and Daniel, named for grandfather and father Sage, are called Hannah and *Joseph Prince*.

Calling "Sara Knight * * * sister-in-law" is, in our modern use of the word, nonsense. Sarah Mascoll married 3 March, 1757, Nath¹ Knight, and if it was her father John, no longer junior, and Hannah (Silsbee) Prince who married 26 Oct., 1739, she may have been a step-sister. She was, in any event, cousin-german.

The will of **13** Nathaniel, p. 15, calls his daughter Hannah Mascoll.

The curious persistence of a family name when once attached to a house may be noted in Dr. Bentley's "Daniels house" although it had been owned and occupied by Silsbees since the deed of gift in 1748, nearly seventy years before.

71 Nathaniel, Salem, is said to have died in New York.

73 Hannah, Salem, XIV,148, 227.

77 Sarah, Salem. Her first husband David Patten, master-mariner, born in 1767, died November, 1805, was an orphan and brought up by her father. He was lost overboard from schooner Bellona, off Hatteras, on a passage from Trinidad, III,176. Haffield White Read was a half-brother of Rebecca Read who married **74** Samuel. She lived in the above-mentioned northern wing of her father's house and was its last Silsbee occupant, thus closing an uninterrupted tenure of 112 years.

49 Nath'l, Salem (**41** W^m, **13** Nathl, **3** Nathl, **1** Henry).

	BORN.	DIED.	MARRIED.	
49 Nathaniel,	9 Nov., 1748,	25 June, 1791,	1 Nov., 1770,	Sarah Becket.

They had

	BORN.	DIED.	MARRIED.	
78 Nathaniel,	14 Jan., 1773,	14 J'ly, 1850,	12 Dec. 1802,	Mary Crowninshield.
79 Sarah,	4 May, 1775,	4 Aug., 1776,		
80 Sarah,	28 Aug., 1777,	12 J'ly, 1840,	12 Feb., 1804,	Tim' Wellman, 4th.
81 William,	21 M'ch, 1779,	15 Jan., 1833,	14 Nov., 1808,	Mary Hodges.
82 Joanna,	21 Sept., 1780,	16 Aug., 1782,		
83 Polly,	28 Aug., 1781,	16 Sept., 1782,		
84 Zac'h Fowle,	9 Aug., 1783,	3 J'ly 1873,	27 Nov., 1810,	Sarah Boardman.
85 Joanna,	22 Sept., 1789,	4 Oct., 1789.		

"At a very early age Mr. Silsbee was entrusted with the charge of a vessel and cargo to the West Indies and subsequently he was the owner of several vessels employed in that trade. * * * He commanded the Grand Turk, on a voyage to the West Indies and afterwards to Spain. * * * He soon acquired what was then considered an independent fortune * * * but, kept on until reverses reduced his estate to a single vessel, in the command of which he once more braved the winds and waves where he had early sought and acquired fortune and fame. * * * At the end of a disastrous voyage, which terminated at New York, his valuable life was closed at the age of forty-three.

His remains were interred in the cemetery of the New Brick Presbyterian Church, fronting the Park." (Geo. A. Ward in "Curwen's Journal," etc., 4th ed., p. 655.)

For Sarah Becket born 15 Feb., 1749-50, died 30 Apr., 1832, see VIII,142.

50 Martha (**41** William, **13** Nathl, **3** Nathl, **1** Henry).

	BORN.	DIED.	MARRIED.		BORN.	DIED.
50 Martha,			1761,	Wm Emmerton,	2 Sept., 1739,	ab' 1762.
			secondly,	Chris' Babbadge.		

They had CHRISTOPHER, WILLIAM, MARTHA, SUSAN.

Wm Emmerton was a son of John and Mary (Foster). He started on a voyage to the West Indies soon after his marriage and was never heard from, XIV,279.

51 JOANNA (**41** W^m, **13** Nathl, **3** Nathl, **1** Henry).

	BORN.	DIED.	MARRIED.	
51 Joanna,			1763,	Mansfield Burrill.
They had	BORN.	DIED.	MARRIED.	
Joanna Burrill,	ab' 1772,	26 Jan., 1853,	13 Nov., 1796,	Henry Webb.
William "	ab' 1767,	20 Aug., 1831,	7 Me'h, 1790,	Eunice Coffrin.
Mansfield "		1837,	18 May, 1794,	Sally Randall.
Martha "			4 Dec., 1785,	Marshall Stocker.
Mary "		1803,		
Sarah F. "		April, 1811.		

Mansfield Burrill born 1 Oct., 1739, died 2 Jan., 1826, son of Ebenezer and Mary (Mansfield) Burrill of Lynn, was a carpenter and built, about 1776, the house on Essex street, next west of the Phillips school house.

54 DANIEL, Boston (**42** Daniel, **36** Henry, **8** Eph'm, **1** Henry).

11 July 1770, he calls himself "Merchant of Boston."

In 1773 the Silsbee family was interested in a claim to a family estate in England. It appears, from a letter from "Dan Silsbee" to Samuel of Salem, dated 22 June of that year, that Samuel had been talking it over with "my brother" (Sampson I suppose) and Dan urges further inquiry to discover the antecedents of our "ancestor Henry Silsbee."

The inquiry was set on foot by "the following extract taken verbatim from the Publick Advertiser 1773." "To Heirs At Law. If any person can prove him or herself to be the real Heirs-at-Law of James Thomas Silsbee— late of Warrendon in the County of Bucks, Esq. deceased—such person by the will of the said James Thomas

Silsbee which is proved in Doctor's Commons, London, is entitled to Wadden Chase in the said county of Bucks and to other considerable estates in the said County of Bucks. Enquire of Mr. Ambrose Reddall."

The following statement, from Lipscombe's History of Buck's, will show on how slight a foundation this dream of wealth rested.

Thomas James Selby, Esq., died in 1772 and in his will (proved 22 Dec., of that year) left his estates to "his right and lawful heir" for the better discovery of whom he directed advertisements to be published, directly after his decease, in some of the public papers; and then added "I do hereby order and direct the legacies to be paid by the said heir * * * within twelve months after my decease; but should it so happen that no heir-at-law is found I, then, hereby constitute and appoint William Lowndes, Esq., my lawful heir and, on condition that he take the name of Selby, I give the estates and all the manors before-mentioned." And the Selby-Lowndes entered upon the estates and, if I mistake not, enjoy them to the present day.

It would be interesting to discover by what accident or by whose design the Thomas James Selby of the original advertisement became changed to the James Thomas Silsbee of the American version.

"Silsby, Daniel, of Boston. An addresser of Hutchinson in 1774. In 1776 he was in England. In 1778 he was proscribed and banished." Sabine's "The American Loyalists," p. 613.

In the "Journal and Letters" of our townsman Samuel Curwen we find Mr. Silsbee dining with him at Governor Hutchinson's; consoling, with a dish of tea at his lodgings, the "old, small, and infirm" judge, after his two hours ineffectual struggle with the crowd at the door of Drury

Lane where they had hoped to see Garrick; adjourning from a disappointing art-exhibition in Piccadilly to the rooms of Joseph Green, wit and poet, where another dish of tea helped "pass a pleasant hour;" and joining "The New England Club," an association of brother-exiles, who dined weekly at the Adelphi, Strand.

He is said to have died in Flanders in 1791, but in an account of guardianship, in Suffolk Probate, B. 98, 550, we find "as per the late Daniel Silsby's will of London."

55 SAMPSON, Boston (**42** Daniel, **36** Henry, **8** Ephraim, 1 Henry).

	BORN.	DIED.	MARRIED.	
55 Sampson,		bef' May, 1824,	24 Sept., 1772,	Abigail Collins.
They had				
86 Enoch,			30 May, 1799,	Alice Needham.

13 March, 1771, John Richards, of Beverly, mortgages some property to Sampson S., of Lynn, but, at his marriage, the next year, he and his wife are called of Boston though married by Ebenezer Burrill, Esq., of Lynn. He lived afterwards at Woburn. 24 May, 1824, Enoch Silsbee says he is next of kin to Sampson S. deceased, intestate, and the balance is paid to "Enoch S., admn'r, son of deceased and sole heir being the only descendant and there living no wife."

Samson Silsby. Wyman Gen. and Est., p. 865.

61 SARAH, Lynn (**43** Samuel, **36** Henry, **8** Ephraim, 1 Henry).

	BORN.	DIED.	MARRIED.	
61 Sarah,	4 June, 1758,	3 Dec., 1820,		Stephen Smith.
They had				
	BORN.	DIED.	MARRIED.	
Daniel Smith,	5 Aug., 1784,	M'ch, 1840,		Lydia Breed.
Stephen "	1 Feb., 1786,	7 Aug., 1860,		Theodate Alley.
			& 2ndly 16 Feb., 1848,	89 Lydia Silsbee.
Samuel "	25 July, 1792,		non-comp.	
Henry "	11 Apr., 1796,	1856,	unm'd.	

Stephen Smith, born in Salem, 25 Sept., 1749, died in Lynn 13 Dec., 1832.

Lydia Breed was dau. of James and Hannah.

63 HENRY, Lynn (**43** Samuel, **36** Henry, **8** Ephraim, **1** Henry).

	BORN.	DIED.	MARRIED.	
63 Henry,	12 July, 1762,	5 Aug., 1821,		Sarah Phillips.
They had				
	BORN.	DIED.	MARRIED.	
87 Content Phillips,	31 July, 1804,	7 Apr., 1846,	26 Oct., 1835,	James Ellis.

Henry, yeoman, is called Blackmarsh Henry, probably to distinguish him from his cousins at Woodend. Silsbee street was laid out through his land. His wife, dau. of Walter Phillips and Content (Hood), was born 30 Dec., 1764, and died 6 Feb., 1835, at Lynn. James Ellis born 1796, died 4 Aug., 1873, and **87** Content Phillips, had one son James H., born 10 Aug., 1838.

64 SAMUEL, Lynn (**43** Samuel, **36** Henry, **8** Ephraim, **1** Henry).

64 Samuel, cordwainer, sells, 28, 3, 1796, to his brother Nehemiah his mansion house at Blackmarsh near that of his father.

His widow, who died 7 March, 1850, aged seventy-three years and seven months, leaves property to her grand-nieces Connor, daughters of Richard son of Jonathan who had married her sister Alice.

65 NEHEMIAH, Lynn (**43** Sam¹, **36** Henry, **8** Ephraim, **1** Henry).

	BORN.	DIED.	MARRIED.	
65 Nehemiah,	12 July, 1768,	3 May, 1832,		Eliz'h Breed.
They had				
	BORN.	DIED.	MARRIED.	
88 Nathan,	21 Dec., 1795,		27 Nov., 1823,	Eliz'h S. Dodge.
89 Lydia	30 June, 1797,	7 M'ch, 1870,	16 Feb., 1818,	Stephen Smith.[7]
90 Samuel,	19 Sept., 1798,			
91 Henry Breed,	19 Aug., 1800,	23 Dec., 1846,	unmarried.	
92 Mary Ann,	29 M'ch, 1805,	9 May, 1860,	"	
93 Elizabeth,	27 Feb., 1811,	14 Oct., 1877,	31 May, 1840,	George Phillips.

---

[7] See **61** Sarah, p. 27.

Elizabeth, his wife, dau. of Nathan Breed and Kezia, dau. of James Buxton of Danvers.

67 HENRY, Lynn (**46** Henry, **36** Henry, **8** Ephraim, **1** Henry).

	BORN.	DIED.	MARRIED	
67 Henry,	24 Apr., 1775,	30 July, 1844,		Mary Chase.
			and secondly	Miriam Gould.
By Mary				
	BORN.	DIED.	MARRIED.	
94 Hannah,	17 June, 1803,	26 Feb., 1877,	31 June, 1827,	Josiah M. Nichols.
95 Mary,	17 Sept., 1806,	24 Sept., 1848,		Wm G. Wentworth.
96 Henry,	14 Sept., 1808,	26 Aug., 1842,		Susannah Upham.
97 Abner,	11 Sept., 1812,		15 Dec., 1836,	Abigail L. Lewis.
By Miriam				
98 Rebecca,	2 Oct., 1818.		22 Jan., 1845,	Luther Williams.
99 Maria C.	22 M'ch, 1820,	17 Apr., 1848,	unmarried.	

67 Henry was a farmer and occupied the old homestead on Fayette street.

Mary Chase was born at Seabrook, Maine.

Miriam Gould born 24 July, 1780, died 16 July, 1857, was dau. of Elihu and Lois.

69 DANIEL, Lynn (**46** Henry, **36** Henry, **8** Ephraim, **1** Henry).

	BORN.	DIED.	MARRIED.	
69 Daniel.	12 May, 1777,	24 Jan., 1840,		Lydia Curtin.
			secondly,	Lydia Nichols.
			& thirdly,	Sally (Curtin) Bur-
By first Lydia				[rill.
	BORN.	DIED.	MARRIED.	
100 Julia Ann,	16 Apr., 1804,			
By second Lydia				
101 Abigail,	26 Jan., 1815,	20 July, 1838.		
102 Lydia Maria,	12 July, 1818,	22 M'ch, 1835.		
103 Hannah Franklin,	15 July, 1821,	24 5–6, 1836.		

Daniel was prominent among the shoe-manufacturers of his time; "with Micajah Burrill made more shoes than all the others combined."

Lydia Curtin, born 23 March, 1784, died 26 Nov., 1812, dau. of John and Sarah.

Lydia Nichols, born 22 Jan., 1790, died 5 Nov., 1822, dau. of Thomas and Hannah of Salem.

Sally Curtin, born 13 Dec., 1787, died 17 Nov., 1831, dau. of John and Sarah, and widow of Micajah Burrill.

100 Julia Ann married David Kent of Salem, their dau. Anna Maria married William Varney of Salem.

74 SAMUEL, Salem (**47** Samuel, **39** Nathl, **13** Nathl, **3** Nathl, **1** Henry).

	BORN.	DIED.	MARRIED.	
74 Samuel,	ab' 1763,	June, 1822,	1 Oct., 1786,	Rebecca Read.

They had

	BAP'D.	DIED.	MARRIED.	
104 Martha,	22 M'ch. 1787,		5 Jan., 1806,	David Beadle.
			& secondly	Asa Hood.
105 Mary,	10 May, 1789,	25 June, 1791,		
106 Rebecca,	13 M'ch, 1791,	10 May, 1862,	14 July, 1811,	John M. Peck.
107 Nathaniel,	29 Dec., 1793,	14 Sept., 1816,		
108 Mary,	22 May, 1796,	4 M'ch, 1797,		
109 Samuel,	27 May, 1798,			Mary Sullivan.
110 John,	13 July, 1800,	28 Aug., 1815,		
111 Sarah,	12 Dec., 1802,	17 Oct., 1849,	10 June, 1821,	Thos. R. Peck.

Samuel, carpenter and farmer, may be said to have brought down to our age the life of the early settlers. He not only eked out the returns of his trade in town by the cultivation of his outlying acres "in the fields," but, sometimes at least, resorted to water-communication and, with less reason than in the olden time when every household had its "water-carriage," went from house to farm by boat.

These North-field lands, whose first purchase we noted in 1684, were held in common from 1803 till after the death of his mother Martha, and then in 1818 divided by lot between her three heirs. I find Sarah Reed selling a part of hers in 1823, the Silsbee heirs in 1835, and the

Sage heirs in 1836; making about 150 years of posses-
sion and descent by inheritance.

109 Samuel married Mary Sullivan and had a dau. who
married Job Curtis and had children, Jobella, Job and
Enoch.

75 DEBORAH, Salem (**47** Samuel, **39** Nath¹, **13** Nath¹,
3 Nath¹, **1** Henry).

	BORN.	DIED.	MARRIED.
75 Deborah,	19 Apr., 1767,	13 Apr., 1836,	8 Oct., 1786, Daniel Sage.

They had

		BORN.	DIED.	MARRIED.
John	Sage,	14 July, 1787,	31 Dec., 1858.	
Hannah	"	24 Oct., 1789.	4 Oct., 1795.	
Daniel	"	9 Nov., 1791,	30 Sept., 1795.	
Joseph Prince	"	9 Feb., 1793,	26 Sept., 1795.	
Hannah	"	23 Jan., 1797.	29 May, 1800.	
Daniel	"	21 Nov., 1798.	30 May, 1802.	
Deborah	"	3 Dec., 1800.	28 Aug., 1802.	
William	"	25 Sept., 1803,	19 M'ch, 1838.	
Mary Ann	"	1 Apr., 1805,		8 J'ne, 1826, Eph'm Emmerton.
Martha Silsbee	"	9 Sept., 1807,	26 Oct., 1808.	
Sarah	"	17 Oct., 1809,		28 Oct., 1828, Chas. F. Putnam.
Margaret	"	17 Dec., 1811,		June, 1839, Edw'd Putnam.

Daniel Sage, master-mariner, born at Greenock, Scotland, 16 March, 1759, died at Salem 18 May, 1836,
III,177. He was well placed in the roll of shipmasters
who, in the early days of American commerce, carried
the name and fame of Salem ships to the remotest port
of rich India.

I have a draft dated Quiberon, 18 July, 1795, for
£3,425. 17. 2., signed by the Comte Joseph de Puisaye,
Gen. en Chef, "in favour of Daniel Sage; he having furnished provisions to that amount, for the army under my
command." About 1802–3 he superintended the building,
at Danversport, of William Gray's ship Laurel (of 425
tons and fourth in size of Salem ships in those days) and
took her to India.

He lived in the Silsbee house, corner of Essex and Daniels streets, in its northern wing, for nearly thirty years after marriage, and then built the house nearly opposite on Essex street (No. 54 in 1874), where he passed the rest of his life, and which his heirs sold to the late Benjamin Webb.

Ephraim Emmerton born 6 July, 1791, died 22 March, 1877, XIV,277.

78 NATHANIEL, Salem (**49** Nath¹, **41** Wᵐ, **13** Nath¹, **3** Nath, **1** Henry).

	BORN.	DIED.	MARRIED.
78 Nathaniel,	14 Jan'y, 1773,	14 July, 1850,	12 Dec., 1802, Mary Crowninshield.

They had

	BORN.	DIED.	MARRIED.
A daughter,	13 Sept., 1803,	15 Sept., 1803.	
112 Nathaniel,	28 Dec., 1804,		9 Nov., 1829, M. A. C. Devereux.
113 Mary C.,	10 Apr., 1809,		21 May, 1839, Jared Sparks.
114 Georgianna,	27 Jan., 1824,		30 Mc'h, 1846, F. H. Appleton.
			2nd, 12 Sept., 1855, Henry Saltonstall.

"Nathaniel Silsbee, born 14 Jan'y, 1773, commenced fitting for Harvard College, by the Rev. Dr. Manasseh Cutler at Hamilton, when nine and a half years old.

After four years he was compelled by pecuniary reverses to leave school, and at fourteen years of age commenced the life of a seaman.

At the end of six years, having made seven voyages to the East and West Indies, and having accumulated nothing for himself, he was given the command by Elias Hasket Derby of a new ship and sailed for the East Indies, being then under twenty and his mate under twenty-one years of age.

The result of this voyage, in a ship of 162 tons and with a stock of $18,000, was the return in nineteen months of two ships with full cargoes of East India productions.

He made many voyages of much adventure and great risk successfully, until, at the end of 1804, he left the sea.

Engaging actively in commerce he took a leading part in everything relating to it, being one of the founders of the Massachusetts Life Insurance Company, and a member of most of the commercial institutions of the city of Boston. He was one of the half-dozen shipmasters who established the East India Marine Society of Salem, and its first treasurer. He was, together with all his and his wife's connections, a member of the East Society under the charge of the Rev. Dr. William Bentley.

They were all Jeffersonian republicans and supporters, with all their means, of the government, in the war of 1812 with England.

At the close of the war he was elected, against his wishes, to a seat in the House of Representatives in Congress, and the residue of his life was given to the public service. He remained in the House from March, 1817, to 1821, and declined a re-election; was sent to the State House of Representatives in 1821.

In 1823 he was chosen to the Senate of Massachusetts and was made its president, to which office he was elected three successive years, when, in 1826, he announced his intention to retire from all public offices. He was, however, unexpectedly notified of his election as a Senator in Congress, to supply a vacancy for four years, and at the expiration of that term was re-elected for another full term of six years, making a senator's life of ten years. He declined a further election and retired to private life in March, 1835.

He was twice chosen a member of the Electoral College for the choice of President.

He was one of the commissioners appointed by the President of the United States to receive subscriptions

3

34

to the United States Bank, and was a director, either in
the Bank at Philadelphia or the Branch at Boston, until he
sold his stock before voting, as a Senator, for its re-charter.

In politics, a conservative and whig through his long
term of service in both houses of Congress, he was looked
up to by all parties for information on business subjects
and treated with universal respect, and regret for his resig-
nation.

He twice received from his constituents the compliment
of a public dinner.

During the recesses of Congress his house at Salem
was visited by Members from all parts of the Union, and
the representatives of foreign governments who came to
New England.

In his later days he took little active part in politics
and they were passed, for the most part, quietly at home."

He lived in his father's house on Daniels street and
afterwards in the mansion, which he built on the northerly corner of Pleasant and Briggs streets (No. 16 on
chart of 1874 and owned by Mrs. E. D. Kimball), where
he died.

Mary Crowninshield, born 24 Sept., 1778, died 20
Sept., 1835, was dau. of George and Mary (Derby),
III,162.

81 WILLIAM, Salem (**49** Nath¹, **41** Wᵐ, **13** Nath¹, **3** Nath¹,
1 Henry).

	BORN.	DIED.	MARRIED.	
81 William,	21 Mc'h, 1779.	15 Jan'y, 1833,	14 Nov., 1808.	Mary Hodges.

They had

	BORN.	DIED.	MARRIED.	
115 Margaret H.,	24 July, 1810,	8 July, 1829.		
116 Benjamin H.,		22 Feb., 1880,	22 Oct., 1840,	Eliz'h J. White.
117 William,	17 May, 1813,		21 M'ch, 1838,	Charlotte Lymon.
			30 M'ch. 1858,	Maria Woodward.
118 John Henry,	17 June, 1814,		15 May, 1838,	Rebecca A. Dodge.
119 Mary,	8 Sept., 1816,			M. Fenollosa.
120 Hannah H.,				
121 Harriet Eliz.,	29 June, 1819,			John N. Mott.

81 William "was an active, intelligent and enterprising merchant, an upright and respected citizen and in all the relations of life esteemed, and his loss will be deeply felt and lamented." (Salem Register, 17 Jan., 1833.)

He lived in the Hodges' house on the eastern corner of Orange and Essex streets.

Mary (Hodges) born 24 May, 1789, died 31 Aug., 1851, dau. of Benjamin, born ab' 1754, died 13 Apr., 1806, and Hannah (King).

84 ZACHARIAH F., Salem (**49** Nath¹, **41** Wᵐ, **13** Nath¹, **3** Nath¹, **1** Henry).

	BORN.	DIED.	MARRIED.
84 Zachariah Fowle,	9 Aug., 1783,	8 July, 1873,	27 Nov., 1810, Sarah Boardman.

They had

	BORN.	DIED.	MARRIED. 1330521
122 Francis Henry,	6 Sept., 1811,	19 Nov., 1848,	
123 John Boardman,	10 Apr., 1813,	1 Apr., 1867,	12 May, 1849, Martha Shepard.
124 Sarah Ann,	18 June, 1814,		19 M'ch, 1846, J. W. Peele.
125 Zachariah,	4 Sept., 1815,	27 Sept., 1815,	
126 Elizabeth,	29 Nov., 1816,	15 Sept., 1817,	
127 Elizabeth,	5 Dec., 1817,	3 Jan'y, 1821,	
128 Caroline,	24 Aug., 1819,		13 June, 1849, Wm. D. Pickman.
129 Mary B.,	3 Jan'y. 1821,		17 June, 1861, Rev. D. Clapp.
130 George Z.,	23 Jan'y. 1822,		16 Dec., 1852, E. S. Saltonstall.
131 Edward A.,	18 Dec., 1823,	soon.	
132 Edward A.,	19 Feb., 1826.		

84 Zachariah Fowle was, after retiring from the sea, always a resident of Salem. Was for many years engaged in foreign commerce with the firm of Stone, Silsbees and Pickman. "He had an uncommonly modest and retiring disposition, which, without doubt, deterred him from wishing to assume any prominent public position; but he filled several offices of trust — such as Trustee and President of the Salem Savings Bank, Director of the Merchants Bank and of the Newmarket

Manufacturing Company. He was a man of the strictest integrity, most amiable, kind and tender-hearted, always charitable to the poor and liberal in all his dealings." ("S" in Salem Gazette.)

86 ENOCH, Boston (**55** Sampson, **42** Daniel, **36** Henry, **8** Ephraim, **1** Henry).

86 Enoch married 30 May, 1799, Alice Needham of Salem; they had **133** Alice married Stephen Emmons; **134** Caroline married Benjamin G. Ropes and was lost in the Arctic, off Cape Race, September, 1854, VIII,54; **135** George Enoch, married Hannah Wells; **136** Sarah Needham; **137** Emma married Thorndike Procter and died 15 Aug. 1877, and **138** Emeline.

86 Enoch for some time after his marriage kept a shop in Salem. In 1809 he was in business in Savannah, Georgia. He afterwards resided in Boston and Roxbury, Mass.

88 NATHAN, Lynn (**65** Nehemiah, **43** Sam'l, **36** Henry, **8** Ephraim, **1** Henry).

	BORN.	DIED.	MARRIED.	
88 Nathan,	21 Dec., 1795,		27 Nov., 1823,	Eliz. S. Dodge.

They had

	BORN.	DIED.	MARRIED.	
139 Catherine,	28 May, 1824,		9 Aug., 1840,	Nathan Mower.
140 Mary P.,	16 May, 1826,		31 M'ch. 1844,	Edw. A. Lummus.
141 Sarah Elizabeth,	22 Sept., 1828,		22 Sept., 1850,	John P. Woodbury.
142 Frances Ellen,	18 Sept., 1830,		1 Jan., 1857,	James H. Nourse.
143 Chas. Frederic,	15 May, 1837,		17 June, 1860,	Anna R. Austin.
144 Nathan Everett,	24 Aug. 1843,		19 June, 1867,	Sarah E. Alley.

Nathan has passed most of his long life in Lynn. He spent two years at the west about 1830. He was a shoemaker but might well have been a real-estate agent, since his keen memory of such matters has often been of great value in settling contested points, and was very useful to myself in confirming the family lines as I had constructed them from deeds, *etc.*

Anna R. Austin was born in Salem, dau. of Henry and Elizabeth (Palfrey).

90 SAMUEL, Lynn (65 Nehemiah, 43 Sam'l, 36 Henry, 8 Ephraim, 1 Henry).

	BORN.	DIED.	MARRIED.	
90 Samuel,	19 Sept., 1798,			Huldah M. Ingalls.
They had				
145 Otis Ingalls,	2 Aug., 1847,		1872,	Jane Mitchell.
146 James Breed,	2 June, 1849,		7 Sept., 1872,	Clara E. Phillips.
147 George Alfred,	22 Feb., 1853,		10 Oct., 1877.	Mary E. Madison.

Samuel, mariner and fisherman in early life, when, for a time, he lived at Nahant, has since been a shoemaker and now, 1878, resides, in hale old age, on Burchsted Court in Lynn.

Huldah M. was daughter of Alfred and Huldah Ingalls of Bridgton, Cumberland County, Me.

93 ELIZ'H, Lynn (65 Nehemiah, 43 Samuel, 36 Henry, 8 Ephraim, 1 Henry).

	BORN.	DIED.	MARRIED.	
93 Elizabeth,	27 Feb., 1811,	14 Oct., 1877,	31 May, 1840,	George Phillips.
They had				
	BORN.	DIED.	MARRIED.	
George H. Phillips,	13 Mc'h. 1841,		31 Aug., 1870.	
Edward N. "	17 Feb., 1844,	25 Dec., 1846.		
Edward "	5 Feb., 1848,	5 Sept., 1848.		
Arthur J. "	18 Jan., 1852.			

Mr. George H. Phillips, of Lynn, furnishes the following sketch of his paternal line. George, born 27 Feb., 1805, died 3 Apr. 1857, was son of John, born 30 Dec.,

1760, died 19 Nov., 1835, and Judith Dow from New
Hampshire, born 7 Jan., 1766, died 8 Oct., 1850; he
was son of Walter, born 17 Sept., 1726, died 18 M'ch,
1800, and Content Hood, born 4 Sept., 1732, died 11
Aug., 1805 (see p. 282); he was son of Jonathan, died
1751, and Mary; he was son of Walter, died 1733, and
Ruth; he was son of Walter (an early settler of Maine
and driven to Massachusetts in 1689 by the Indians),
whose will is dated 21 Oct., 1704, and Margaret whose
will is dated 8 Nov., 1708.

94 HANNAH (**67** Henry, **46** Henry, **36** Henry, **8** Eph'm,
1 Henry).

Hannah, born 17 June, 1803, died 26 Feb., 1877, married Josiah M. Nichols, born in Salem, son of Stephen
and Abigail (Moulton). Their children were: Mary
Silsbee, born 2 May, 1828, married 1st, Elias T. Pulsifer,
2nd, Henry Coombs; Henry Silsbee, born 7 Feb., 1830,
married, 1849, Elizabeth, dau. of John Thompson of
Marblehead; Stephen, born 28 May, 1832, died 9 Sept.,
1833, and Jonathan Conner, born 10 Dec., 1834, died
15 Sept., 1835.

96 HENRY (**67** Henry, **46** Henry, **36** Henry, **8** Eph'm,
1 Henry).

96 Henry, born 14 Sept., 1808, died 26 Aug., 1842,
married 12 Nov., 1833, Susannah, dau. of Asa and Ruth
(Richardson) Upham of Melrose, Mass., born 25 Feb.,
1809. Their children were: **148** Henry Otis, born 6
Aug., 1837, and **149** Edwin, born 28 Oct., 1840, died
23 Apr., 1842.

Henry was a farmer and lived with his father on Fayette street.

97 ABNER, Lynn (**67** Henry, **46** Henry, **36** Henry, **8** Ephraim, **1** Henry.

	BORN.	DIED.	MARRIED.	
97 Abner,	11 Sept., 1811,		15 Dec., 1836,	Abig'l L. Lewis.
They had				
	BORN.	DIED.	MARRIED.	
150 William Lewis,	12 Sept., 1837,			
151 James Albert,	11 Nov., 1839,	17 Apr., 1848.		
152 Abbie Maria,	6 Mc'h, 1841.		13 July, 1859,	Andrew Mace.
153 Alden Burrill,	15 Aug., 1845,	22 M'ch, 1849.		
154 Sylvester,	24 Jan., 1848,	12 Apr., 1849.		
155 Charles Albert,	5 May, 1850.		6 Aug., 1873,	Althea L. Shaw.

Abner lives on Fayette street, not far from the location of **1** Henry.

Abigail L. Lewis, born 8 Nov., 1813, was dau. of James F. and Abigail (   ) of Lynn.

Althea Louise Shaw, born in Lynn 15 Apr., 1852, was dau. of Benjamin Franklin and Lucretia Leland (Burrill) Shaw.

98 REBECCA (**67** Henry, **46** Henry, **36** Henry, **8** Eph'm, **1** Henry).

Rebecca, born 2 Oct., 1818, married 22 Jan., 1845, Luther Williams, born in Concord, Me., 22 Oct., 1818, died in Solon, Me., 23 Apr., 1870. Their children were: Summer G., born in Lynn 12 Nov., 1845, married 31 Oct., 1873, in North Vassalboro, Ella F. Wyman. They reside (1877) in Lewiston, Me. Maria S., born in Lynn 6 May, 1849, died in Solon, Me., 3 Aug., 1865. Henry S., born in Lynn 26 Feb., 1851; Mary Ann F., born in Lynn 14 Jan., 1853, died in Lynn 20 May, 1859; Alden B., born in Lynn 6 Nov., 1856, died in Lynn 21 Nov., 1859.

In a letter dated Solon, Maine, 22 April, 1878, she writes "I have some earthen plates that they brought over from England with them." These are, perhaps, remnants of the "Delph ware" mentioned in the inventory of **36** Henry.

106 REBECCA, Cincinnati (**74** Sam¹, **47** Sam¹, **39** Nath¹, **13** Nath¹, **3** Nath¹, **1** Henry).

		BAP'D.	DIED.	MARRIED.
106 Rebecca,		13 M'ch, 1791,	10 May, 1862,	14 July, 1810, John M. Peck.

They had

		,BORN.	DIED.	MARRIED.
John M.	Peck,	10 Feb., 1812,		9 Apr., 1839, Eliz'h S. Fithian.
Thomas R.	"	11 M'ch, 1813.		
Mary S.	"	7 July, 1814.		
Thomas R.	"	13 Apr., 1816.		
Rebecca Ann	"	8 Aug., 1817.		
A son	"			
Sarah Maria	"	2 June, 1820.		
Emily Prince	"	17 Nov., 1821,	7 Sept., 1867.	4 May, 1847. Nath¹ R. Stout.
Edward Augustus	"	25 May, 1823,		28 Dec., 1847. Marg¹ S. Bowling.
Alex'r Gregory	"	12 Nov., 1824.		12 Sept., 1848, Sarah McKee.
Adel' Augusta	"	12 Jan., 1827.		23 Oct., 1849, Benj. R. Wilson.
Augusta Amanda	"	6 Sept., 1828,		14 Sept., 1847, Edw. J. Wilson.
A son	"	3 May, 1833.		

John M. Peck died 19 Feb., 1867. Eliz. S. (Fithian) died 31 M'ch, 1868. Sarah (McKee) died 28 Feb., 1871. Edward J. Wilson, 12 Nov., 1872.

111 SARAH, Medford, Mass. (**74** Samuel, **47** Samuel, **39** Nath¹, **13** Nath¹, **3** Nath¹, **1** Henry).

		BORN.	DIED.	MARRIED.
111 Sarah,		6 Dec., 1802,	11 Oct., 1839,	10 June, 1821, Thomas R. Peck.

They had

		BORN.	DIED.	MARRIED.
Hannah G.	Peck,	11 Ap., 1822,	14 Nov., 1854,	2 Ap., 1854, Albert F. Sawyer.
Harriet R.	"	5 June, 1823,		9 Dec., 1840, Sam'l T. Thompson.
Sarah Rebecca	"	10 Jan., 1825,		15 Ap., 1857, David G. Ranney.
Mary Elizabeth	"	21 Sept., 1826,		12 Aug., 1862, James A. Hervey.
Lucy Amelia	"	24 Jan., 1828.		
Margaret Sage	"	29 Nov., 1830.		
Thomas R.	"	16 Nov., 1832,	13 May, 1855.	
Caroline Augusta	"	3 June, 1836,	15 Ap., 1837.	
Julia Anna	"	3 June, 1836,	31 Mc'h, 1837.	
Julia Augusta	"	22 Ap., 1838.		16 Sept., 1856, Samuel K. Leach.
Fred' Silsbee	"	20 Ap., 1839,	8 May, 1841.	

Thomas Ressigiue and John Morris (**106**) Peck came from Connecticut. They were hatters. Thomas R. for many years kept a hat-store in Boston and a hat-factory in Medford, where he still (1880) resides.

112 NATHANIEL, Salem (**78** Nath¹, **49** Nath¹, **40** Wᵐ, **13** Nath¹, **3** Nath¹, **1** Henry).

	BORN.	DIED.	MARRIED.
112 Nathaniel,	28 Dec., 1801,		9 Nov., 1829, M. A. C. Devereux.
They had	BORN.	DIED.	MARRIED.
156 Nathaniel D.,	22 Oct., 1830,		22 Oct., 1856, Mary S. Hodges.
157 George D.,	29 Oct., 1832,	18 Aug., 1843.	
158 Eliza D.,	23 Oct., 1835,	20 M'ch, 1837.	
159 Marianne D.,	11 Sept., 1837,	10 M'ch, 1838.	
160 Mary C.,	7 Apr., 1840,		12 June, 1861, F. A. Whitwell.
161 Wm. Edward,	27 Sept., 1843.		

"Nathaniel Silsbee * * graduated at Harvard College in 1824, and settled in Salem.

He was elected to the House of Representatives of Massachusetts for the session of 1833, and again for that of 1846, and, subsequently, for the extra session of three days in 1848, called to cast the Presidential vote of the State, which was given to Zachary Taylor.

Although earnest in his politics, which were conservative, he was disinclined to political office, but was much interested in municipal affairs and was elected by the *Whig party* Mayor of Salem in 1849, and again in 1850, when he declined a reëlection and served a year in the board of Aldermen.

Having passed some years in Europe, he was, on his return, elected by the *citizens* Mayor for the year 1858 and again in 1859, when he again declined a reëlection.

In 1862 he was chosen Treasurer of Harvard College and removed to Boston.

He served in that capacity for over fourteen years, and then resigned the charge of that Trust.

In 1869 he became a citizen of the town of Milton, passing his winters in Boston."

Mary Anne Cabot Devereux, born 6 Feb., 1812, was dau. of Humphrey.

He built and occupied the house on the southerly corner of Pleasant and Andrew streets (No. 17 on chart of 1874) till after the death of his father, whose house he occupied till his removal to Boston.

113 MARY CROWNINSHIELD, Salem (**78** Nath¹, **49** Nath¹, **40** Wᵐ, **13** Nath¹, **3** Nath¹, **1** Henry).

	BORN.	DIED.	MARRIED.	
113 Mary C.	10 Apr., 1809,		21 May, 1839,	Jared Sparks.

They had

		BORN.	DIED.	MARRIED.	
Mary C.	Sparks,	29 May, 1842,	25 June, 1842.		
Florence	"	28 Oct., 1845,		16 Nov., 1876,	Benj. P. Moore.
Wm. Eliot	"	23 Oct., 1847,		20 Jan., 1874,	Harriet A. Mason.
Elizabeth W.	"	1 May, 1849,		9 M'ch, 1876,	Ed. C. Pickering.
Beatrice	"	26 M'ch, 1851.			

Jared Sparks born in Wellington, Conn., 10 May, 1789, died at Cambridge, Mass., 14 M'ch, 1866. Was graduated at Harvard College, 1815. Unitarian pastor at Baltimore, Md., May, 1819. McLean Professor of Ancient and Modern History, Harvard College, 1839–1849. President Harvard College 1849–52. See Hist. and Gen. Reg., XX, 272.

114 GEORGIANNA (**78** Nath¹, **49** Nath¹, **40** Wᵐ, **13** Nath¹, **3** Nath¹, **1** Henry).

By her first husband had son Frank H. Appleton (born 17 June, 1847, married 2 June, 1874, Fanny R. Tappan. They had dau., Marianne, born 14 M'ch, 1876) and, by her second husband, son Gurdon Saltonstall, born 15 Aug., 1856, died 21 May, 1878.

116 BENJAMIN H., Salem (**81** W^m, **49** Nathl, **41** W^m, **13** Nathl, **3** Nathl, **1** Henry).

	BORN.	DIED.	MARRIED.
116 Benjamin H.		22 Feb., 1880,	22 Oct., 1810,	Eliz'h J. White.

They had **162** Elizabeth W., **163** Margaret and **164** Francis.

"The death of this estimable gentleman, which occurred on Sunday forenoon, in the 69th year of his age, leaves a void in our community which will be widely and deeply felt. Mr. Silsbee had long been one of our most valued, respected and influential citizens. Descended on both parental sides from the successful pioneers of American commerce, he was born into the advantages of competency, a liberal education, and an assured social position. To these advantages were added healthful natural tendencies which preserved him from all evil influences, and carried him through, from the beginning to the end, a pure and exemplary life.

In his political and religious convictions Mr. Silsbee was very firm, decided, and outspoken; and on no point did he ever shrink from frankly declaring his convictions. His religious faith and his parish church he loved, and cherished their welfare with all his heart. His party (the Republican), he supported earnestly in all that he believed to be right, and as earnestly opposed whoever and whatever seemed to be corrupting to its purity. He had, however, a repugnance to the holding of political office, and resisted the requests which were often made to him to become a candidate. In our local charities he was always prominent, and faithfully performed the important duties which he had accepted in connection with many of them.

Mr. Silsbee had been out of health for nearly a year past, but his final sickness was very brief, commencing with pneumonia, one week previous. He was a son of the late William Silsbee, and graduated at Harvard University in the class of 1831, with the historian, John Lothrop Motley, Rev. John H. Morison, Wendell Phillips, N. R. Shurtleff and other distinguished men.

After Mr. Silsbee's graduation he entered upon a business career, sailing in the employ of the old firm of Stone, Silsbee & Pickman, of which the present firm is an offshoot, as supercargo in the famous old ship Borneo, making two voyages, returning in 1838. In 1839 he entered the firm, which at about that period commenced to build its own ships. He continued in active business from that time until his decease. He took a generous interest in all that appertained to the well-being of Salem. For the last sixteen years he had been President of the East India Marine Society, of which his grandfather, Benjamin Hodges, was the first President. Mr. Silsbee was also President of the Merchants' National Bank, the Salem Lead Company, and of the Association for the Relief of Aged and Destitute Women; and, until quite recently, also of the Salem Savings Bank, besides being an officer in the Newmarket and other manufacturing companies. He was a member of the East (Unitarian) Church, and for many years was Superintendent of its Sunday School. He was a member of the Board of Aldermen in 1859, and also at one time a very efficient member of the school committee. He had repeatedly been solicited to accept the candidacy for the office of Mayor, but firmly declined the proffered honor." (Salem Gazette).

He lived on the eastern corner of Oliver and Brown streets.

Elizabeth J. is dau. of Rev. John White of Dedham, Mass., son of Deacon John White of Concord, Mass., where he was born 2 Dec., 1787. He was graduated at

Harvard College, 1805, ordained pastor of the Third Church in Dedham 20 April, 1816, and died there 1 Feb., 1852.

117 WILLIAM, Trenton, New York (**81** W^m, **49** Nathl, **41** W^m, **13** Nathl, **3** Nathl, **1** Henry).

	BORN.	DIED.	MARRIED.	
117 William,	17 May, 1813,		21 M'ch. 1838,	Charlotte Lyman.
			30 M'ch, 1858,	Maria Woodward.

By Charlotte he had

	BORN.	DIED.	MARRIED.	
165 Annie Jean,				
166 Henry Bellows,		in infancy.		
167 Joseph Lyman,	25 Nov., 1818,		5 June, 1875,	Anna B. Sedgwick.

"**117** William, H. C., 1832. Ordained at Walpole, N. H. Seventh minister over the "Town Congregational Society," 1 July, 1840. Resigned this ministry in 1842. Preached successively in Newport, R. I., in Cabotville (now Chicopee), Mass., and in Troy, N. Y., for periods of five to ten months each. From 1851 to 1853 taught a private school in Cincinnati. In the summer of 1853 went to Europe. Returned in September, 1854. In April, 1855, accepted a call to the pastorate of the Second Congregational Church in Northampton, where he remained as Pastor till May, 1863, when he resigned his charge. From 1863 to 1867 resided in Cambridge. In 1868 (June 1st) was settled as minister of the "Reformed Christian Church" in Trenton, New York, where he has since remained.

Charlotte Lyman, daughter of Erastus and Rachel (Hutchins) Lyman, was born at Norwich (now Huntington), Mass., Oct. 16, 1814, and died Nov. 29, 1848.

Maria P. Woodward, daughter of Samuel B. and Maria (Porter) Woodward, was born in Wethersfield, Conn., Aug. 3, 1826."

118 JOHN HENRY, Salem (**81** W^m, **49** Nathl, **41** W^m, **13** Nathl, **3** Nathl, **1** Henry).

	BORN.	DIED.	MARRIED.	
118 John Henry,	17 June, 1814,		15 May, 1838,	Rebecca A. Dodge.
They had				

	BORN.	DIED.	MARRIED.	
168 William Hodges,				
169 Alice Dodge,	31 Oct., 1843.		1 Dec., 1864,	Hall Curtis.
170 Walter J.,		July, 1868.		

118 John Henry, II. C., 1832. Is a merchant in Salem. He lives in the house on Essex street numbered 380 in the chart of 1874.

Rebecca Ann, dau. of Pickering and Rebecca (Jenks) Dodge, born 21 Dec., 1819. XV,301.

119 MARY and Manuel Fenollosa had Ernest Francisco, H. C. 1874, married Elizabeth G. Millett and is now a Professor in the Tokio University, Japan; and William Silsbee, H. C. 1875, temporary instructor in music at Harvard in 1879.

Manuel Fenollosa, son of Manuel and Isabel (del Pino), was born at Malaga, Spain, 24 Dec., 1822; was a music-teacher in Salem, where he died 13 Jan'y, 1878. See "Kinsman Family," p. 201.

121 HARRIET ELIZABETH and John N. Mott had a dau. Mary.

122 FRANCIS HENRY, Salem.

"Was graduated at Harvard in 1831. Entered upon the practice of the law; but, in about a year—Oct., 1835—became Cashier of the Merchants' Bank in Salem, in which post he died, unm'd, 'after a long and lingering illness.'" Hist. and Gen. Reg., V,159.

"He was modest, unobtrusive and retiring; fond of

belles lettres and the fine arts, he felt himself unfitted for the bustle of his profession and accepted the position which he faithfully filled to the time of his death." (Salem Gazette, 19 Nov., 1848).

123 JOHN B., Salem (**84** Zach. F., **49** Nathl, **41** W^m, **13** Nathl, **3** Nathl, **1** Henry).

	BORN.	DIED.	MARRIED.
123 John Boardman,	10 Apr., 1813,	1 Apr., 1867,	12 May, 1849, Martha Shepard.

They had

	BORN.	DIED.	MARRIED.
171 Emily Fairfax.	7 June, 1850,		1 June, 1871, Am'y A. Lawrence.
172 Arthur Boardman,	19 Jan., 1854.		
173 Martha,	4 Nov., 1859.		
174 Thomas,	10 Oct., 1863.		

John Boardman, Harv. Coll., 1832, was a merchant.

He built and occupied the house on North street (No. 6 on the chart of 1874), and bought the Pickman house on western corner of Chestnut and Pickering streets, where he died.

124 SARAH ANN, Salem (**84** Zach. F., **49** Nathl, **41** W^m, **13** Nathl, **3** Nathl, **1** Henry).

	BORN.	DIED.	MARRIED.
124 Sarah Ann,	18 June, 1814,		19 M'ch, 1846, J. Willard Peele.

They had

	BORN.	DIED.	MARRIED.
Willard S. Peele,	19 Nov., 1847,		
Jane A. "	8 Dec., 1848,		15 May, 1873, Walter Hunnewell.
Mary S. "	7 Apr., 1850,		2 June, 1870, Daniel A. Dwight.

J. Willard Peele, son of Willard and Margaret (Appleton), died at his seaside residence in Beverly, 29 Sept., 1871, aged 67. He established the house of Peele, Hubbell & Co., at Manilla. In Salem he lived on Chestnut street, No. 14, atlas of 1874.

128 CAROLINE, Salem (**84** Zach. F., **49** Nath¹, **41** Wᵐ, **13** Nath¹, **3** Nath¹, **1** Henry).

	BORN.	DIED.	MARRIED.
128 Caroline,	24 Aug., 1810,		13 J'ne, 1840, W. D. Pickman.

They had

	BORN.	DIED.	MARRIED.
Dudley Leavitt Pickman,	23 Dec., 1850.		
Fanny P.	"	30 May, 1857, 6 Oct., 1880,	31 Oct., 1877, Wm. F. Wharton.

William Dudley Pickman, son of Dudley L. and Catherine (Sanders), is a merchant for some years residing in Boston. XV,303.

129 MARY B., married 17 June, 1861, "*Rev. Dexter Clapp*, who died of consumption July 26, 1868.—He was son of Ralph and Fanny Clapp, born in Westhampton, Mass., 15 July, 1816; graduated at Amherst College, 1839, Divinity School, Cambridge, 1842; ordained as an Evangelist in New York city in 1843, and immediately after stationed at Savannah, Ga.—In December, 1846, he succeeded Rev. Theodore Parker as pastor of 3d Cong. Ch. in West Roxbury, and was called thence to become colleague pastor with Rev. James Flint, East Church, Salem, and was installed 17 Dec., 1851, resigned on account of ill-health, 19 Jan'y, 1864. "Mr. Clapp's pastorate in Salem was a most beautiful and most acceptable one. * * He was one of the most charming and beloved of men, of clear mind and earnest heart, acceptable everywhere as a preacher, and combining the humility and devoutness of the true disciple with the unction and fervor of an apostle. His father was a New England Farmer."

"Mr. Clapp's first wife Susan F., dau. of Judge Preston, born in Bangor, died in Salem, of cancer, June 21, 1859, aged 42, and was buried in Mt. Auburn."

130 GEORGE Z., Salem (**84** Zach. F., **49** Nath¹, **41** Wᵐ, **13** Nath¹, **3** Nath¹, **1** Henry).

George Z., born 23 Jan., 1822, married 16 Dec., 1852, E. S. Saltonstall. They had **175** George S., born 21 Aug., 1854, **176** Catherine E., born 14 Sept., 1856, and **177** Frank B., born 28 May, 1867.

George Z. is a merchant in Salem and Boston. He built the house on the northwestern corner of Flint and Warren streets, where he has since resided. Elizabeth Sanders Saltonstall was born 26 May, 1825, dau. of Nathaniel, born 1 October, 1784, died 19 October, 1838, and Caroline (Sanders).

135 GEORGE E., Bradford, Mass. (**55** Sampson, **42** Dan¹, **33** Henry, **8** Ephraim, **1** Henry).

A farmer and married Hannah Wells. They had **178** Emily A., married B. S. Clough of Salisbury, **179** George E., **180** Sara Ella and **181** Edward.

140 MARY P., Lynn (**88** Nathan, **65** Nehem^h, **43** Sam¹, **36** Henry, **8** Ephraim, **1** Henry).

	BORN.	DIED.	MARRIED.
140 Mary,	16 May, 1826,		31 M'ch, 1844, Edw. A. Lummus.

They had

	BORN.	DIED.	MARRIED.
Edw. Flint Lummus,	24 M'ch, 1847,	21 Jan., 1868,	unm'd.
George "	6 Jan'y, 1849,	6 Sept., 1865,	unm'd.
Eola M. "	6 M'ch, 1851.		Chas. A. Ramsdell.
Mary S. "	11 June, 1855.		
Eliot J. "	2 May, 1858.		

Edward A. Lummus was born 8 Feb., 1820, died 8 Jan., 1862.

141 SARAH E., Lynn (**88** Nathan, **65** Nehem^h, **43** Sam¹, **36** Henry, **8** Ephraim, **1** Henry).

Sarah Elizabeth, born 22 Sept., 1828, married 22 Sept.,

4

1850, John P. Woodbury. They had Marcia E. Woodbury, married Edward P. Parsons, and John W. Woodbury.

John P. Woodbury was born May, 1827, in Atkinson, N. H., son of John, jun.

142 FRANCES E., Lynn (**88** Nathan, **65** Neh[h], **43** Sam[l], **36** Henry, **8** Ephraim, **1** Henry).

Frances Ellen, born 18 Sept., 1830, married 1 Jan., 1857, James H. Nourse. They had Ellen Frances Nourse, born 22 Nov., 1865, and Florence B. Nourse born 23 Nov., 1870.

James H. Nourse, son of John and Emma B. (Sprague), is foreman in the shoe-factory of G. W. Downing on Monroe street in Lynn.

144 NATHAN EVERETT, Lynn (**88** Nathan, **65** Nehem[h], **43** Sam[l], **36** Henry, **8** Ephraim, **1** Henry).

	BORN.	DIED.	MARRIED.
144 Nathan Everett,	24 Aug., 1843,		19 June, 1867, Sarah E. Alley.

They had

	BORN.	DIED.	MARRIED.
182 Walter E.	6 July, 1868.		
183 Charles W.	1 M'ch, 1871,	9 M'ch, 1878.	
184 Grace E.	13 Oct., 1874,		

N. Everett Silsbee has been since 1857 in the Real Estate and Insurance business, firm of Silsbee and Pickford, Union street, Lynn.

Sarah Ellen Alley, born 18 Feb., 1843, in Lynn, dau. of Timothy and Sarah Alley.

145 OTIS INGALLS, Lynn (**90** Sam[l], **65** Nehem[h], **43** Sam[l], **36** Henry, **8** Ephraim, **1** Henry).

Otis I., shoefinisher in Lynn, and Jane, dau. of Joseph and Abby Mitchell of Kittery, Maine, had **185** Emma

Mabel, born 1 Nov., 1873, **186** Harriet Mitchell, born 1875, and **187** Philip Samuel born 1877.

146 JAMES BREED, Lynn (**90** Sam[l], **65** Neh[h], **43** Sam[l], **36** Henry, **8** Ephraim, **1** Henry).

James B., Real Estate and Insurance Broker in Lynn, and Clara Emma, dau. of William T. and Emily S. Phillips, of Bangor, Maine, had **188** Emily Alice born 20 Feb., 1877.

148 HENRY OTIS, Lynn (**96** Henry, **67** Henry, **46** Henry, **36** Henry, **8** Ephraim, **1** Henry).

148 Henry Otis married 3 Oct., 1861, Cordelia A., dau. of Dudley and Cynthia (Smith) Chandler, born 13 May, 1841. They had **189** Henry born 24 M'ch, 1862. He is a farmer tilling and occupying some of the land bought by his immigrant ancestor in 1651.

152 ABBIE MARIA, born 6 M'ch, 1841, married 13 July, 1859, Andrew Mace born in Reedfield, Maine, about 1831. They had Frank W., Andrew, Arthur, Charlotte E.

156 NATH'L D., Boston (**112** Nath[l], **78** Nath[l], **41** Nath[l], **40** W[m], **13** Nath[l], **3** Nath[l], **1** Henry).

	BORN.	DIED.	MARRIED.	
156 Nathaniel D.,	22 Oct., 1830,		22 Oct., 1856,	Mary S. Hodges.
They had				

	BORN.	DIED.	MARRIED.	
190 Eliza W.,	27 Sept., 1857,		Aug., 1876,	W. L. Montgomery.
191 Nathaniel,	9 Feb., 1859.			
192 Rosamond W.,	16 Nov., 1863.			
193 George D.,	30 Dec., 1865.			

Nathaniel Devereux, Harvard College, 1852.

Mary S., dau. of George A. and Abigail E. (White) Hodges, VII,201.

190 Eliza W. and W. L. Montgomery had Hugh Devereux, born April, 1877.

160 MARY CROWNINSHIELD, born 7 Apr., 1840, married 12 June, 1861, Frederic Augustus Whitwell, born 10 M'ch, 1820. They had Frederic S. Whitwell, born 12 M'ch, 1862, and Natalie S., born 2 July, 1863.

167 JOSEPH LYMAN (**117** W^m, **81** W^m, **49** Nathl, **41** W^m, **13** Nathl, **3** Nathl, **1** Henry).

Born in Salem, Nov. 25, 1848. Married in Syracuse, June 5, 1875, Anna B. Sedgwick, dau. of Charles B. Sedgwick of Syracuse, by whom he has three children : **194** Charlotte, **195** Margaret, **196** Joseph Lyman, jr.

He was graduated at H. C., 1869. "Studied as an Architect in Boston ; spent more than a year in Europe, from 1872 to 1873 ; went to Syracuse, N. Y., in the latter year, where he has ever since found employment as an architect, besides his work in Albany and other parts of the State, and to some extent outside the State."

169 ALICE DODGE (**118** John H., **81** W^m, **49** Nathl, **41** W^m, **13** Nathl, **3** Nathl, **1** Henry).

Alice Dodge, born Oct. 31, 1843, married Dec. 1, 1864, Hall Curtis. They had John Silsbee Curtis, born Oct. 18, 1865, and Fanny Mixter Curtis born M'ch 28, 1870.

Hall Curtis, son of Nathaniel and Emily Matilda (Hall)* Curtis, born July 7, 1834. Harvard College, A. B., 1854 ; M. D., 1857 ; M. M. S. S. Ass't Surgeon 24th Mass. Vol. Inf. ; Surgeon 2nd Mass. Art'y ; Visiting Physician, Boston City Hospital, 1871.

---

* See Brooks Hist. Medford, p. 517.

SUPPLEMENTARY NOTES.

TOMPKINS, RALPH, p. 7.

Suffolk Deeds, Lib. 1, 91.

Know all men by these presents that I, Raph Tomkins of Salem, have sold unto John Farnham, of Dorchester, his house and home lot with a ten Acre lot abroade in the woods, with all his right in the Commons (for and in consideration of XXXIX li.) to him and his heirs forever. With warrantie of the same dated 2 (4), 1648.

Witness, Wm. Phillips. —— Raph Tomkins marke.

SILSBEE, JONATHAN, pp. 12, 13.

The following facts, furnished by Mr. John Silsby of Bucksport, Maine, give, there is little doubt, some of the descendants of 6 Jonathan.

John Silsby, born 30 Aug., 1782, at "Scotland, Windham County, Conn' probably," had a brother Bliss Silsby, since of Bath, Maine; a brother Ahial, lost at sea; and sisters, one named "Roxy."

Towards the end of 1801 John married Sophia, dau. of Elisha Avery, born 1 Jan., 1757, married 12 April, 1777, at Norwich, Conn., and died 10 Feb., 1807. His wife Sibbel (Sanger) died at Woodstock, Conn., 7 Jan., 1865, "almost a centenarian." After the death of Sophia, John married, about 1824, her sister Sibbel, who lived to her ninety-seventh year.

John Silsby and Sophia (Avery) had

	BORN.	DIED.	MARRIED.
Charles,	22 Dec., 1802,	29 Nov., 1817.	
Henry,	6 Sept., 1804.	11 Feb., 1852,	Mary Handy Pease.
Lucy,	26 Oct., 1806,	10 Oct., 1821.	
Abby Bliss,	13 Aug., 1808,	16 Dec., 1817.	
John.	5 May, 1811,		2 Dec., 1833, Frances A. Lanpher.
			10 July, 1867, Mary A. H. Whitmore
Samuel Abbott,	30 Nov.,·1813,	29 Sept., 1814.	
Samuel Abbott,	10 Apr., 1816,	15 Nov., 1817.	
Wm Bliss,	23 Sept., 1818,	18 July, 1847.	
Sophia,	17 Sept., 1820.	3 Apr., 1851,	1 Jan., 1843, Emery Cady.
Emily,	11 May, 1823,	26 Aug., 1823.	
Emeline,	11 May, 1823,	26 Feb., 1873,	22 Aug., 1855, Emery Cady.

John Silsby, sen., was a hatter; he lived in Norwich, Conn., where the first four children were born; in Woodstock, Conn., where the other children were born and where all died (except Henry who died at sea on his way from Bucksport, Maine, to San Francisco), and at Plainfield, Conn.

John Silsby, jun., born 5 May, 1811, is a grocer at Bucksport, Me., where he married 2 Dec., 1833, Frances Ames, dau. of Anson and Hannah (Ames) Lanpher. His second wife, Mary Ann (Heath), in her sixty-fifth year, 1880, was widow of Joseph Whitmore of Verona, Hancock Co., Maine.

John and Frances had John Alonzo, born 25 M'ch, 1835, married Elvira Josephine Munson and lives at Olympia, Washington Territory; Frances Ellen, born 3 April, 1838, died 16 May, 1839, and Charles Hobart born 8 Oct., 1844, and died 14 Dec., 1862. These births and deaths happened at Bucksport, Maine.

SAGE, JOHN, p. 23.

John Sage was a school-teacher at Greenock, Scotland, where, beside Daniel, he had a daughter Catherine who married a McCrea and emigrated to North Carolina. She had two married daughters before 1801. By a second wife, John had daughters Ann and Isabell, who, as well as their mother, were living at Greenock in 1801.

John Sage, tobacconist, of No. 335 Sauchichall street, Glasgow, has traditionary knowledge of descent from Greenock, and beyond that from the shores of Loch Fine; but the Greenock parish registers, at Edinburgh, singularly failed to confirm either line.

SPELLING OF SURNAME.

It will, possibly, be worth while to collate all the forms used in this sketch : Sellesby, Scylesbie, Sillsbey, Sillsby, Silsbey, Silsby, Silsbee, Silsbye and Sylsbe. To these may be added Scilsbey, Silsbe, Sillsbe and Sillsbee. All these I have seen. Any other combination of letters, giving essentially the same sound, would give little surprise to one familiar with the audacious ingenuity of our ancestors in such matters. As a rule, by no means without exception, the descendants of **3** Nathaniel write Silsbee; all others Silsby.

METHOD OF ENUMERATION.

It will be observed that its own distinguishing number has been retained for each of the christian names of a man's direct paternal ancestors: *i. e.*, those names, in brackets, following the name of the head of the family in each family-history.

This avoids the confusion resulting under the common method of giving only a generation number, whenever the same christian name is used more than once in a generation.

The index-table, giving his distinguishing number and page to each head of a family, will, it is hoped, enable those least familiar with such matters, to trace their own descent readily; and, with a little study, ascertain the degree of relationship in the various lines.

GRADUATES OF HARVARD COLLEGE.

Appleton, Francis H.,	1842.	Saltonstall, Leverett,	1802.
Appleton, Francis H.,	1869.	Sawyer, Albert F.,	1849.
Clapp, Dexter,	1842.	Silsbee, Arthur B.,	1875.
Curtis, Hall,	1854.	Silsbee, Benjamin H.,	1831.
Devereux, Humphrey,	1798.	Silsbee, Francis H.,	1831.
Fenollosa, Ernest F.,	1874.	Silsbee, George S.,	1874.
Fenollosa, William S.,	1875.	Silsbee, John B.,	1832.
Hervey, James A.,	1849.	Silsbee, John H.,	1832.
Hunnewell, Walter,	1865.	Silsbee, Joseph L.,	1869.
Lawrence, Amory A.,	1870.	Silsbee, Nathaniel,	1824.
Montgomery, W.,	1867.	Silsbee, Nathaniel D.,	1852.
Moore, B. P.,	1871.	Silsbee, William,	1832.
Peele, Willard,	1792.	Silsbee, William E.,	1867.
Pickering, E. C.,	1865.	Wharton, William F.,	1870.
Pickman, Dudley L.,	1873.	White, John,	1805.
Saltonstall, Henry,	1848.		

THANKS.

I take this opportunity to acknowledge my obligations to all who have assisted me in this compilation: especially to Mr. Henry F. Waters, of Salem, for most essential help in arranging the earlier generations; to Hon. Nath'l Silsbee of Boston; to Rev. William Silsbee of Trenton, New York; to Mr. George S. Silsbee of Salem; and to Messrs. N. Everett Silsbee and J. M. Nichols of Lynn, for facts in their respective lines.

INDEX.

INDEX-TABLE

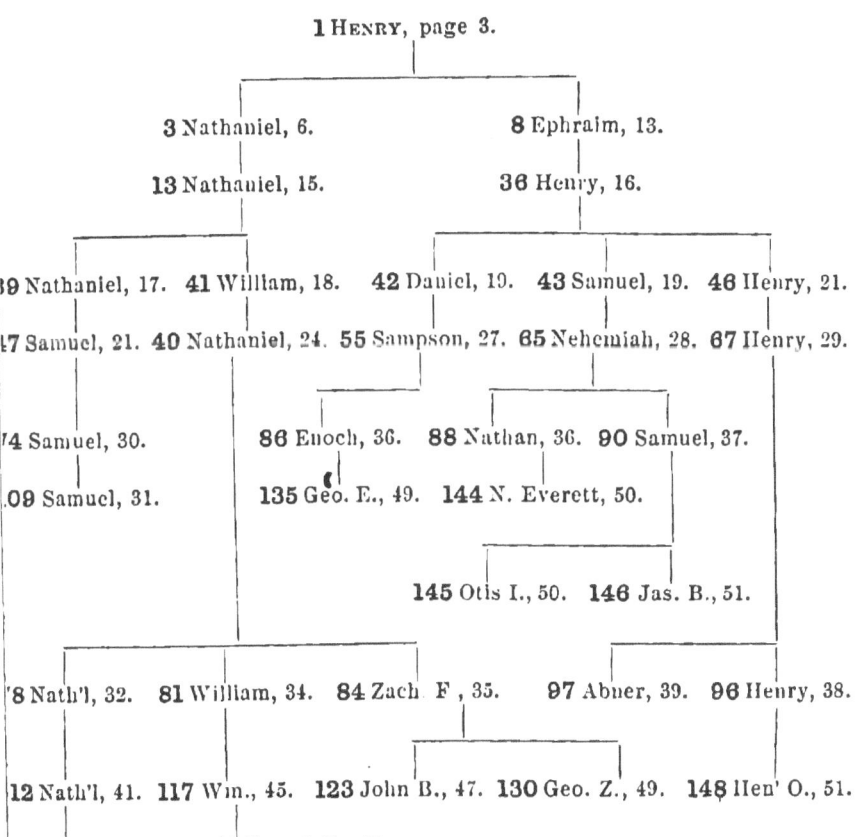

INDEX.

(61)

Hatteras, 23.
Hawks, 20.
Heath, 54.
Heires, 20.
Hervey, 40, 56.
Higginson, 17.
Hoag, 21.
Hodges, Abigail E., 52.
    Benjamin, 34, 44.
    George A., 52.
    Hannah, 34.
    Mary, 24, 34.
    Mary S., 41, 51, 52.
Hood, Asa, 30.
    Content, 28, 38.
    Sarah, 14.
Hubbell, 47.
Hunnewell, 47, 56.
Huntington, 45.
Hutchins, 45.
Hutchinson, 26.

Ierson, 5.
Ingalls, Alfred, 37.
    Huldah, 37.
    Huldah M., 37.
Ingersoll, 18.
Ipswich, 4, 5.
Ipswich river, 7.
Ives, 9.

James, Enoch, 10.
    Francis, 11.
Japan, 46.
Jenks, 46.
Johnson, 13.

Kent, 30.
King, 35.
Kinsman, 46.
Kimball, 34.
Kittery, Maine, 50.
Knight, Sara, 22, 23.
    Nathaniel, 23.

Kyrtland, 4.

Lanpher, 54.
Larned, 12.
Laughton, Thos., jr., 14; sen., 15.
Laurel, ship, 31.
Lawrence, 47, 56.
Leach, 40.
Leland, 39.
Lewis, Alonzo, 6, 15, 20.
    Abigail, 39.
    Abigail L., 39.
    James F., 39.
Lewiston, Maine, 39.
Lilly, 12.
Linn, 5.
Lipscombe, 26.
Loch Fine, 55.
London, 3, 26, 27.
Lowndes, 26.
Lummus, Eola M., 49.
    Eliot J., 49.
    Edward A., 49.
    Edward F, 36, 49.
    George, 49.
    Mary, 36, 49.
    Mary S., 49.
Lyman, Charlotte, 34, 45.
    Erastus, 45.
    Rachel, 45.

Mace, Abbie M., 39, 51.
    Andrew, 39, 51.
    Arthur, 51.
    Charlotte E., 51.
    Frank W., 51.
McCrea, 55.
McGregor, 21.
McKee, 40.
Madison, 37.
Malaga, 46.
Maine, 38, 53, 54.
Manila, 47.
Mansfield, 25.

www.ingramcontent.com/pod-product-compliance
Lightning Source LLC
Chambersburg PA
CBHW030025030726
47499CB00008B/3127